Only Earl In The World

Only Earl In The World

AMALIE HOWARD

A Taming of the Dukes Novel

Publisher: RAH Media, LLC

Identifiers: ISBN 978-1-967784-00-4 (ebook), ISBN 978-1-967784-01-1 (paperback)

Book cover design and art by Rut Bisbe

First edition 2025

FALL IN LOVE WITH AMALIE HOWARD

"Refreshing, steamy, and stocked with characters you don't normally get to see in the genre—her books are a must-read for me."
— Jodi Picoult, #1 *New York Times* bestselling author

"Amalie Howard tells a story with self-assured style, wit, and energy. Her writing sparkles!"
— Lisa Kleypas, #1 *New York Times* bestselling author

"The fresh voice historical romance needs right now . . . I will read every word she writes."
— Kerrigan Byrne, *USA Today* bestselling author

THE WORST DUKE IN LONDON

"Howard's appealing, forward-thinking female characters enliven this equally sensual and emotional love story. Readers won't want to put it down."
— *Publishers Weekly*

"Splendidly entertaining . . . a wickedly witty, sublimely sensual love story inspired by the classic rom-com, 10 Things I Hate about You."
— *Booklist*

"Howard's writing brings the chemistry between her characters to life, and the book is compellingly written. A sexy romp for readers who enjoy charming historical romances with modern sensibilities."
— *Library Journal*

"Fans of 10 Things I Hate About You and historical romance are in for a treat. Filled with funny banter, memorable characters and spicy moments, this Regency-era love story delights!"
— *Woman's World*

NEVER MET A DUKE LIKE YOU

"[A] page-turning Victorian romance . . . Howard's admirable and progressive protagonists and Clueless-inspired plot are sure to have readers charmed."
— *Publishers Weekly*

"A sizzling dance of seduction. Combine this with a thoughtfully developed, neurodivergent heroine and an intriguing plot that offers insights into the attempts to reform the treatment of mental illness in the Victorian era, and you have a love story that is both smart and sexy."
— *Booklist*

"A bright, charming love story of childhood friends and second chances with shades of Jane Austen and the '90s rom-com Clueless . . . snappy dialogue and simmering sexual tension, doing justice to the story as a romance and as an homage to a romantic comedy classic."
— *Library Journal*

ALWAYS BE MY DUCHESS

"A dreamy summer romance designed to sweep you up into a world of ballerinas, hunky dukes, cheeky girl gangs, and delicious sex scenes. Light on angst and heavy on charm, it's a feel-good read of the highest order."
— *Entertainment Weekly*

"The story slayed me from page one."
— *Paste Magazine*

"Howard creates great characters and dialogue . . . A real treat."
— *Library Journal*

"Howard's lyrical writing enlivens her bright, empathetic characters and her sharp eye on their class and cultural disparities only enhances their romance. Readers will be riveted."
— *Publishers Weekly*

"Fabulous writing . . . such a delicious escape. Utterly delightful!"
— Eloisa James, *New York Times* bestselling author

TAMING OF THE DUKES

Always Be My Duchess
Never Met a Duke Like You
The Worst Duke in London

CONTENT GUIDANCE

Mental health issues, including postpartum depression, are discussed. There are mentions of sex work and sex workers as well as consensual sexual situations, including references to brothels, toys, and flagellation. Period-specific terms such as pimp, harlot, and courtesan are used in context. Abuse, assault, weapons, and death are described. Profanity is used in narration and dialogue.

For those who shipped Briar and Lushing from the start, this one's for you.

CHAPTER ONE

Lady Briar Fairview was in a dastardly pickle.

Slightly more dastardly than usual, she amended in her head as her gaze narrowed on the two unwashed and gin-soaked men who had cornered her into a filthy, small alleyway.

Venturing into Seven Dials in disguise among the cutpurses and the pimps was a regular outing so that she could identify and help young girls who found themselves in dire circumstances through no fault of their own. Facing off against dissolute drunks was not, however. Her plain, dark, and male clothing usually helped to keep her invisible, but her luck had turned tonight. Perhaps they'd only stumbled after her by mistake.

A girl could hope, but better to be safe than sorry.

Assumptions in this neck of the woods got people killed.

Briar reached beneath her cloak and closed her fingers around the pocket pistol she always carried...not that she'd ever had to use it, despite being an excellent shot. Shooting a person and shooting clay targets at her father's ancestral seat in Surrey were two vastly different things. One was living and breathing, after all.

She cursed the crooked nail on the doorjamb of the tavern she'd been in that had wrenched her hat from her head, along with a handful of pins holding her mass of tight, corkscrew curls in place. She'd thought she might have escaped notice, but to her dismay, the two men had stayed on her heels.

She could not afford to be recognized.

This wasn't Surrey or Bath, and she was no longer sixteen and wild. A peeress in London crossing the bounds of patriarchy-stamped propriety had to be cautious or risk being sent to a convent, married off without her consent, or even incarcerated in an asylum for, God forbid, hysteria. Thank heavens, she was affianced to a very appropriate, well-respected gentleman.

Who would probably forbid you to set foot in St. Giles if he had any inkling...

Briar grimaced at the thought. She had been neighbors in Surrey with Preston and his older brother for years until Preston had left for a three-year stint at a priory in Italy. When he had succeeded the viscountcy after his brother had died without any children and approached her father over the winter, no one in her family had been surprised that he'd tendered an offer of marriage.

He was an even-tempered, titled suitor with a reasonable offer. He would be a tolerable spouse, and their relaxed, neighborly friendship would continue.

It was *perfect* for her needs.

Besides, everyone at home had predicted they would marry eventually, and at least Preston was a devil she knew.

*Hardly a devil...*more like a saint with a stick—several sticks —lodged firmly up his arse. The quiet boy she remembered had transformed somewhat after his return from the Italian abbey. He'd made small barbed comments here and there about decorum, chiding her fondness for expletives.

She did curse quite a lot, thanks in part to her best friend Vesper, though admittedly, they both enjoyed using words forbidden to women. In truth, in their world, excessive swearing could get a girl committed. Especially under the aforementioned affliction of hysteria...

Vesper's fiancé, the Duke of Greydon, was focused on bettering the current lunacy laws. His father had been committed by his mother under false pretenses, and the duke had died because of inhumane treatment. Vesper had told her over tea a few weeks ago that Greydon had shown her a report from an asylum in the United States where some men had committed their female relatives for asinine reasons like Novel Reading and Imaginary Female Trouble. While it was hardly a laughing matter, they had snorted over the supposed maladies men had invented to get rid of their spouses, like Deranged Masturbation.

As if self-pleasure were a crime or one worthy of such severe punishment.

Good God, she and the rest of the Hellfire Kitties would be locked away until the end of time. They all firmly believed in the power and agency of their own sex.

Menstrual Deranged had been another reason for involuntary admission to an asylum. Men were so terrified of women's courses that they'd invented a disease to account for the simple manifestation of one's God-given bodily functions. Hysteria was no joke, having been documented by many male physicians as the root cause of eccentric or erratic behavior, should any young lady take one step out of line.

In high society, female purity, propriety, and politesse were the admirable pillars of a virtuous and true woman.

Horseshit, if anyone asked Briar.

Women were complex creatures, and purported purity did not make one more valuable than the other. Fallen women, as the *ton* loved to refer to them, weren't any less. They were simply people who had made different choices, whether they were deliberate or not. Some women, like the ones she helped, had plummeted into hard times through no fault of their own—the death of a family member or even the loss of employment because they hadn't groveled to a man. Briar's lip curled over her teeth in disgust.

Those women weren't *fallen*; they were victims of circumstance.

And such misfortune could happen to everyone.

But tell that to any man who believed he was deserving of unspoiled goods in a wife...simply because that was what women had become: commodities. In their world—the upper echelons of the *ton*—virginity was lauded and bartered like gold. Briar refused to let something like a tiny flap of skin, which didn't even exist for all women according to modern medicine, determine her worth.

Preston would not care how she came to the marriage bed. After all, *he* had never been a monk. She bit her lip, remembering his latest remarks about her virtuous and moral comportment. Or would he?

Then again, now wasn't the time to dwell on the moral constitution of her fiancé.

She had more immediate problems.

Briar cleared her throat and deepened her voice to try to imitate a man. "Oy, lads. I'm warning you! Come any closer and you'll taste a mouthful of lead. Begone with you!"

One of the men smiled, teeth blackened and missing in spots. "What's a pretty gel like you doing in a place like this?" he slurred, making Briar's heart sink. Damn and blast!

Bravado would only do so much if they thought her a man. The minute they pinned her for a woman, it would make her easier prey in their eyes. It was an innate superiority that came with most men of their ilk; they thought themselves stronger, hardier, wiser. More fool them. But growing up with four stepbrothers who had always idolized but underestimated her, Briar had driven herself to be as good as or better than they had been.

To be fair, her father had indulged her rather unconventional whims, even though the youngest of her stepbrothers was ten years older than her. She'd been taught how to fence, box, and shoot, she'd had tutors in the same subjects they studied, and she'd learned never to back down with a bully.

Or *bullies* in this case.

"No gel here," she said in a deep voice, pulling herself up to her full height. She was a woman, not a girl, and neither of those made her weak or anyone's quarry.

"A gent with such pretty hair?" the other man said, and Briar cursed silently. "Give us a look, little moll."

"Last chance," she warned them, but they only laughed.

Her odds of escape were slim but not impossible. Nothing was *impossible*, though escape might take some finessing or creativity. Or brute strength. She rolled her neck. The dank alley was blocked with rubbish at the far end, and the two men standing nearly abreast took up the only way out. On the one hand, they were drunk, and she was not. She was small and quick, and if the opportunity arose, she could dart between them and run. Lastly, if push came to shove, she was armed, and she would fight tooth and nail.

Swearing through her teeth, Briar clenched her jaw and cocked the pistol in its holster, the sound loud in the silence of the night, letting them know she meant business. A gunshot would be even louder and draw more attention than she needed. If word got back to her father, it wouldn't only be her reputation in danger...she'd be locked away with the key thrown to oblivion.

The brigands narrowed the gap between them, close enough now that their unwashed stench overwhelmed her nostrils. Every muscle in Briar's body readied for flight or fight. Noiselessly, if she could help it. She did not want to end up in the scandal rags. Her professions—both in fact—were better conducted incognito.

"Stay back, you scoundrels, I'm warning you!"

They ignored her, triangulating their positions so one man was on each side of the alley. Bloody hell, they weren't *that* foxed then. "Easy, pretty filly. Why don't you come over and play nice with old Jack and Tommy?"

Filly? Play nice? Briar's blood boiled. Why was it that men had this idea of women that they had to come to heel when bidden like a well-trained dog? Even drunken sots who looked like they hadn't seen a comb or soap in an age...as if it was their right to take what *wasn't* on offer?

"Because you stink," she couldn't help snapping. "And I'm not nice."

It was entirely the wrong thing to say, but then again, Briar wasn't known for her ability to filter her thoughts.

Their gazes hardened, grins widening at what she'd revealed. That she was not, in fact, a man.

She grinned back, baring her teeth in a deranged snarl. Briar didn't care—her hands were just as capable in men's or women's gloves. She flung the sides of her cloak to the side, displaying the weapons belt beneath, her cocked and loaded pistol tucked into its holster on one side, and a very sharp epee on the other. A small brace of daggers sat in a girdle at her waist.

"Still want to play, little toads?" she taunted, and without waiting for an answer, threw one of the daggers at the accomplice on the right. The sharp blade caught him in the shoulder, and he stumbled back into the wall with an agonized howl.

Briar didn't hesitate; she charged forward, ducking the clumsy swing of the primary assailant, before smashing him in the temple with the butt of her weapon. He slumped down and went out like a light. A muffled curse alerted her to the attack from behind as the first man she'd wounded rushed her, pure humiliated rage on his face.

Briar sideswiped him and then pointed the muzzle right at his head with the utmost confidence. "I didn't blow your brains out, so leave while I'm feeling generous," she hissed, seeing him gulp as the stench of urine filled the air. He'd pissed his pants in fear. "But first, I'm going to need my dagger back, if you please."

"Who are you?" he yelped as she leaned forward to pluck the blade from his flesh with her free hand, a grimace wrinkling her nose. She'd stitched up many a wound, seen more blood in these filthy back streets of Seven Dials than any lady could imagine, and the sight of the blood-darkened blade still turned her stomach. She wiped it on his already gin-stained coat.

"No one to you, now bugger off before I change my mind," she said, watching as he turned and bolted, leaving his unconscious friend on the ground.

"Well, that's that then," she said, uncocking the gun and replacing it in the holster. Briar didn't know if the man was going to come back with any more of his friends to teach her a lesson or some such. She wouldn't put it past him, even though she'd let him go. Male pride was a fragile devil of a thing.

A low, rich chuckle met her ears.

Oh, hell.

Briar straightened and froze at the sight of a figure leaning against a guttering lamppost across from the mouth of the alley, arms folded over his chest. The onlooker wasn't drunk, nor was he loud. He was dressed in an elegant suit of dark clothing, and he only watched her like a hawk, head tilted to one side as she approached with each step from the alley.

Was he one of the many pimps who frequented this part of town?

Who preyed on desperate women and girls?

But the gentleman tipped his chin up, the light bleeding onto the auburn waves and the sharp angle of a much-too-handsome face beneath his top-hat as Briar let out an unladylike oath. Damn and blast her terrible luck. She'd have much preferred if it'd been a pimp. Or more thieves. A dozen of them, in fact! But no.

Of course, it had to be *him*.

Jasper Lyndhurst, the useless Earl of Lushing. Her

unwanted soldier of the bodyguard, nemesis, partner, and an excruciating pain in her goddamned arse.

"Bloody hell," she swore.

An impish smirk curled one corner of a pair of much too full lips as the vainglorious redhead tutted. "Sweetbriar, is that you?" he drawled. "I couldn't quite see your face in the alley, but that blade-sharp, vicious tongue of yours...well, it's a dead giveaway."

She ground her molars together at the nickname. "That's not my name, you brainless oaf, and clearly, you know it's me."

"Do you prefer Thorny then? Poison Ivy? I am also partial to Prickles."

"None of them because you know my name is Briar," she spat, ignoring the jolt of alarm at the second suggestion—it was much too close to a certain secret nom de plume. "What are you doing here? Were you standing there observing the whole time? Did you not think to help when I was trapped by two deuced meaters who could have killed me?"

Perhaps she was being a tad histrionic, but who cared?

The earl pushed off the post and rolled his wide shoulders. "But you did not need my assistance, did you? It looked like you were doing just fine."

He closed the distance between them and loomed over her, but she stood her ground, keeping her face neutral. Like her, he was dressed in black trousers, a dark waistcoat and coat. A scent of warm leather, cedar, and the crisp night air clung to him, doing aggravating things to her insides that she should not think about. *Would not* think about. She was an engaged woman now, after all. The trifling flirtations over the past few years would have to stop.

"It was quite a show actually," he said. "I enjoyed watching you in action. Don't worry, I wouldn't have let anything happen to a single pretty curl on this head." He reached out for a loosened spiral that hung below her chin and tugged playfully on it.

"Glad to entertain," she said drily, her neck going hot for no good reason as she yanked her head out of his reach, wincing at the tight pull of her hair that was followed by an unspeakable burst of pleasure that struck out of nowhere. Her lungs went on hiatus, leaving her unable to take in a full sip of air for a breathless minute.

Gracious, what would it feel like if he had grasped a handful of the mass in his fist and tightened those long fingers? While he situated her on her knees from *behind*... The ensuing visions, ones of arched spines and gasping breaths, thrusting hips and sweat-dampened skin, were shockingly visceral.

Briar blinked at the scandalous images and sucked in a bracing breath as her temperature spiked. Goodness, was she catching a chill? It *was* unseasonably cold this evening.

Yes, that was it. Not the fact that she was imagining the utterly intolerable *Earl of Lushing* pulling her hair in a manner that was decidedly inappropriate and having fantasies that were better saved for use as inspiration elsewhere. Briar was no stranger to erotic scenes, considering she invented them for a living.

Filing her imaginings away for later, she made the mistake of meeting his gaze, breath hitching anew at the knowing she saw reflected there...as if he could see right through her to the truth of her ribald thoughts. With a hiss of irritation, she pressed a gloved fist over her chest, noting the moment that hooded gaze dropped to the motion, and her breath fizzling when his gaze roved over her bosom, garbed in snug men's clothing.

Something that looked too much like desire flashed in those limpid blue eyes.

Though she had to be mistaken. Perhaps it was disapproval.

Because they loathed each other. Everyone knew it. They could barely go any time at all without snapping or getting into a quarrel. He was the splinter lodged beneath her skin and the perpetual thorn in her side. They were like cats and dogs, oil and water, chalk and cheese. He was a profligate. He was obnoxious. He was a controlling know-it-all.

And yet, he was someone she would trust with her life.

As well as the lives of others...

Briar exhaled a silent sigh. They weren't friends, nor were they each other's intimate tastes. She categorically did *not* fancy much-too-handsome redheads with eyes like the deepest ocean and a lush bedroom baritone that should be illegal. She liked calm, boring gentlemen with good manners and quiet dispositions like Viscount Sackley. He was *safe*, and he would not get in her way. Briar required a husband she could *manage*.

And God alone knew that Lushing was utterly unmanageable.

Besides, the earl had no interest in her...at least not if his usual choice of companions was anything to go by. Jasper Lyndhurst was currently courting a woman who was Briar's complete opposite—meek, quiet, sweet. The flaxen-haired, bright-eyed Lady Penelope Adler was the perfect high society rose. She would make Lushing an impeccable bride. Strange that the idea of him belonging to somebody was not one she'd ever considered.

A fist clenched around Briar's gut, for no good reason.

She scowled. The earl's matrimonial plans were no business of hers.

Indeed, it was truly a wonder that she and Lushing worked so well together, despite their volatile temperaments. Then again, Briar suspected she was one of the few people who ever got a glimpse of the real man behind all the many, *many* masks he loved to wear, and even those sightings were rare. In that regard, Lady Penelope was perfect for him. She would never dig deeper than he allowed, never incite him to anger or passion, never take up any more space than he was willing to give.

The similarity of their comparable prospects did not escape Briar's notice.

Predictable. Easy. Uncomplicated.

Dull.

The thought of her own future husband inexplicably set her teeth on edge before she shook her head hard. Uninspiring and governable were what she wanted. *Sackley* was who she needed. Not a man who constantly had her on her toes because he found it diverting to goad her to distraction. Or *follow* her like an annoying Peeping Tom.

"Don't you have your own precious damsel to worry about? Stop pestering me," she groused over her shoulder to the earl. "Can't you leave me alone?"

Enigmatic dark blue eyes caught hers, a hint of ferocity flashing in them. "Good thing you're no damsel, and no, Sweetbriar, I cannot."

CHAPTER TWO

Jasper sank his palms into his pockets, though he longed to drag the gallingly provocative woman back to the safety of Mayfair. God, she was the most infuriating bit of muslin on the planet, and if she wasn't careful, one of these nights, she wouldn't be so fortunate, and she was going to get herself in trouble or killed.

Lady Briar might be the most dauntless lady he'd ever met who could acquit herself with any weapon as well as a man, but she wasn't invincible. Even now, dressed as she was in tight, form-fitting black from head to toe with armaments galore and hair wild and unruly about her shoulders, she embodied a warrior goddess from some ancient culture.

But the capricious chit was *not* immortal—she was made of flesh and blood.

And mortals could die.

So, yes, he was quite serious about not yielding to her commands. If she wanted to gallivant across the risky parts of London, he would never be far behind. Covertly, of course.

It wasn't his duty, Jasper knew, but the thought of any harm coming to her was not something he wanted to entertain. She was one of his sister's best friends, and someone had to look out for her!

Vesper would be inconsolable if Briar were hurt.

Not that the rebellious hellion couldn't handle herself. Briar had four older stepbrothers from her mama's first marriage before her own parents had been wed. Theirs had been a surprising love match, and one so late in life between a widow and a widower that everyone in high society had been astounded. In their world, marriages were alliances to shore up fortunes and titles. Marrying for love was rare. Marrying for love in the sunset of one's life, even rarer.

But Jasper supposed that was love: fickle to a fault.

His entire set all seemed to have succumbed to Cupid's crooked arrow, however. First Montcroix, then Greydon, and more recently, the Duke of Vale. None of his mates had been safe from love's impulsive capers, nor from the women who had snared them. They were all besotted! Even his own sister Vesper had beguiled their childhood friend and neighbor into a proposal. Jasper snorted.

Good thing *he* wasn't looking for an affair of the heart. That was simply too much work, and Jasper liked his life *simple*.

Besides, keeping up with his nemesis's intrigues was a full-time job, which left little time or space for any other strong-willed women. He shook his head. One day, he should just leave the willful harpy to her own devices. Jasper sighed, a dull throb taking up between his temples.

As if he could *ever*.

After seeing her in action, he'd be the first to concede

that the lady was formidable. The youngest of her brothers was an inspector with the Metropolitan Police who had taught her self-defense and how to shoot. That didn't mean she couldn't be hurt, however, as he constantly reminded himself. And if she didn't want to listen to reason, then he would be both shadow and shield. Unwanted or not. God help him if any of his set found out how he spent some, if not most, of his evenings, chasing a reckless brat all over creation.

Another heavy sigh left him. He was the last thing from a hero, but when it came to Briar, his instincts ran disturbingly hot. Even tonight, it had been harrowing to watch those scapegraces corner her like an animal without wanting to burn them to ash. He supposed the protective impulse was strong because she was as dear as a sibling to him. Like Vesper.

Liar. She's nothing like a sister...

Ignoring his know-it-all inner voice, he kept pace with his quarry, letting her heady floral scent fill his nostrils. She smelled like a night-blooming jasmine—sweet and primal in equal measure. It was an earthy yet sensual fragrance, aromatic with a hint of bite, just like her. Even if he did not think of Briar as a sister, nothing could transpire between them. Vesper, his actual sibling, would murder him first, especially if he broke her heart.

And Jasper was quite adept at that skill.

It wasn't *his* fault that women seemed to love him. Well, except for one. He sniffed. *Most* women, then. Briar Fairview was categorically impossible to charm, not that Jasper hadn't tried. The chit was immune to cajolery.

He almost crashed into her, so intent he was on his musings.

"Bloody hell, are you *trying* to smother me, Lord Lushing?" Briar asked whirling around, those silky bronze spirals tumbling willy-nilly about her face. His fingers itched to delve within them, but he mumbled an apology when she resumed walking, and kept his hands firmly buried in his pockets.

The shockingly aroused expression she'd worn for a heartbeat when he'd tugged on the soft, springy curl earlier had made his mind wander to darker, unsuitable places... places a lady like Briar didn't belong.

Besides, she was an engaged woman, and he was about to present his own suit to Penelope's father...thanks in part to *his* own father, The Duke of Harwick, who was claiming to be on his last legs. Jasper was convinced, however, that it was a sneaky ruse to see his son and heir finally off the marriage mart. Supposedly, Jasper's wedding was the duke's most fervent last wish before he cocked up his toes.

Theatrics ran rampant in his family...

That said, a love match might not be in the cards, but wedding vows certainly were. Tying the knot was all part and parcel of aristocratic duty. He was the last remaining eligible bachelor of his set, after all. Despite suspecting his father's ploy, Jasper knew it was time that he made an honest man of himself, especially after Briar's recent announcement. Just as he was the last gentleman standing, she was the last lady in their close-knit circle who wasn't wed.

Had he, somehow, been unconsciously waiting for her?

No, she hated him, as she had expressed many, *many*

times. She had wished him dead more than once and threat-ened to bury him in the backyard. She'd compared him to an in-growing toenail! She had also called him a brainless oaf and swollen-headed, though the innuendo for the last had made for some delightful teasing on his part. She'd *loathed* that.

In truth, Jasper didn't know what a spitfire like Briar saw in the lackluster Viscount Sackley. Rumor had it that the viscount had been on track to become a vicar in Italy before his elder brother died, and he'd been summoned back to England to succeed to the viscountcy. And since a viscount typically required a suitable viscountess at his side, Briar had been his choice.

Jasper gritted his teeth.

The man was a fucking milksop. But perhaps that was the draw—she was angling for a husband who would not meddle or get in her path. However, something about the viscount rubbed him the wrong way. Sackley had always been an oddball with his taciturn nature, but of late, he'd become outspoken in Parliament on the rights and roles of women in a man's world. In other words, they should be seen and not heard, and their opinions should be the same as their husbands. He had voted against several amendments supporting suffrage.

Considering Briar was an active suffragist with very loud and progressive opinions, his thorny little ivy was in for a rude awakening.

Sackley could not handle a woman like her. A man with such stringent views on women certainly would not put up with her gallivanting all over London dressed in men's clothing and equipped with a small armory of weapons or engaging in fisticuffs with local ruffians in back alleyways. In truth, not many men of their acquaintance would, but Jasper had a strong hunch that the viscount would not condone such habits.

She would either run roughshod all over him or he would snuff the light and the laughter from her eyes. Given what he knew about Sackley, Jasper would wager on the latter. The thought galled him, though it was not his place to interfere or intervene. One, Briar would have his hide, and two, she was a grown woman, capable of making her own choices even if *he* didn't like them. *He* had no say.

"So, Viscount Sackley, is it?" he asked her as they marched back in the direction of the main square. "I read the engagement announcement in the paper."

She glanced up, jade-green eyes glinting in the light of a nearby lamp, surprise in them. "Do you know him?"

"We're acquainted, but I wouldn't say I know him well." Jasper folded his hands behind his back. "A bit of a hulver-head, isn't he?"

"As opposed to being an obnoxious, self-aggrandizing, nosy braggart?" she shot back and then blew air through her teeth as if frustrated with herself for responding thus. She cleared her throat. "He's *not* dull, he's quiet and benevolent with a perfectly good head on his shoulders and a perfectly solvent estate. He's a perfectly suitable match for anyone."

Jasper hid his grin. "Are you trying to convince me or yourself, Sweetbriar? That's a lot of perfect in one sentence."

She opened her mouth and closed it in outrage, a rosy blush spreading over her cheekbones that he could admire even in the guttering streetlight. "Don't you have somewhere else to be?" she demanded rudely. "Instead of harassing me about subjects that aren't any of your business?"

"I'm only making conversation."

She huffed. "Well, make it with someone else. Don't you know when you're not wanted? Go soak your head, Lushing."

"How rude! Fine, if you insist, but solve a riddle for me first: what will your perfect viscount think of your nocturnal habits?" Jasper asked when they walked down the street toward the waiting plain black coach sitting outside a tavern. At least she hadn't come on horseback this time—he'd much rather she keep a coachman with her instead of being alone. And he also trusted Olsen.

Though if Jasper ever suggested she take a carriage for safety, he knew she would do the opposite just for spite. Her pettiness when it came to him knew no bounds, and he secretly adored her for it. He liked a bit of sass in his women. Not that Briar was *his*...but he enjoyed the sharpness of her wit and the fact that she kept him guessing.

"Preston won't know," she muttered eventually.

Jasper released a low chuckle. "He won't know that you aren't at home beside him in bed where any dutiful wife should be, begetting the next crop of blue-blooded heirs?"

She gave a sharp inhale, and if he hadn't been paying attention, Jasper would have missed the wrinkle between her brows as if the very thought of bedding her future husband was an eventuality she hadn't considered. "We shall sleep in separate rooms, of course."

"Do your parents sleep in separate chambers?" Jasper asked.

"Well, no, but they're in love," she replied. "This is a

marriage of convenience and suitability. There won't be any of...that."

That...

Jasper couldn't help his smile at her revolted tone. He did not, however, dwell on the fact that the thought of Briar in bed with anyone—much less fucking Sackley—chafed in a way that illogically made him want to break something with his bare hands.

"What about heirs?" he prodded.

One shoulder rose in a dismissive shrug. "I am certain I do not know what you mean, my lord," she said.

Oh, this was too rich. In her haste to deflect, she'd left herself wide open. The little imp absolutely knew what he meant, considering the company they both kept at Lethe with the women who were in the family way and needed their help. A wicked laugh left him. "Well, not that I expected to provide an impromptu anatomy lesson this evening, but when a husband and a wife want to procreate, he puts his co—"

Briar spun so quickly, he barely had time to move before her hand smashed over his mouth. "Don't you dare finish that sentence, you insupportable rogue! I am well-versed in what private appendage goes where, thank you very much."

"Are you?" he taunted, voice muffled against the press of her palm. The scent of her soft skin—that night-blooming jasmine and the salt of her sweat—made his mouth water. He wanted to lick between the creases of her slender fingers. What would she do if he did? He pretended to gnaw at the fingers closed over his mouth, catching the tip on one of them between his teeth, and she yanked her hand away with a gasp.

She glared at him. "It's not as though I don't get enough of an education from the women at Lethe on the intricacies as well as the consequences of seduction and copulation."

"Isn't the *consequence* the whole point?"

Furious green eyes rimmed in thick curling dark lashes flashed up at him, and Jasper was arrested by the faintest silvery glimmer of her freckles over her nose bridge. Usually they were more pronounced, but in the moonlight, they were muted like flakes of snow on her light brown skin.

"Don't be obtuse. Of course I intend to have a family eventually. It's the obligation and duty of every aristocratic heiress, isn't it? Seed our wombs with future generations. Our value as human incubators is well-nigh law." Her blush heightened as the words flew from her in a torrent. Jasper stared, mesmerized. God, he relished her precocity. "And as far as conjugal relations, I assure you, Lord Lushing, you needn't worry your tiny little vacuous brain about it. Besides, I'd wager I know more about the act of coitus than you do, even with all your vast realm of experience."

His nether regions twitched at those provocative words. Riling her up had always been one of his favorite pastimes—it was like a drug he could not get enough of. Those flashing eyes that promised violence and the pouty lips holding back the vilest of insults were like fucking oxygen to him.

"Is that so, Prickles?" he asked in a drawl that was sure to provoke the beast. "That's quite the boast from someone of your...delicate sensibilities."

The challenge dropped between them. Would she back down? Concede the point?

Her mouth opened and closed, and Jasper braced giddily for whatever scathing riposte would leave that razor-sharp tongue. "That *is* so," she said, glowering at him. "And it's no boast at all, regardless of my *sensibilities*. Half the men in the ton have no clue about female pleasure at all. Lie there and think of England. How shortsightedly unoriginal. It's rather selfish on their parts, really."

Jasper captured her wrist and arched a brow, holding her in place before she could flee from him with that devilishly incendiary parting shot and escape into her waiting coach across the street. "Enlighten me, then, oh wise one."

"Pleasure is not a male-limited endeavor," she snapped.

"Nor should it be."

Her nostrils flared. "If I had *my* say, women should always come first."

Surely, she didn't mean...

But the emphasis on *come* as in *climax* was stark. Jasper's breath stuttered, blood already rushing south. Her expression went gloriously defiant as if daring him to contradict her, and he couldn't help it; he smirked with elated disbelief. "I happen to agree wholeheartedly."

"And they should not be afraid to ask for what they want in the bedchamber or out of it. Pleasure should never be a point of shame, whether it's alone or with a partner. It's my hope to change that with every story I—*ballocks*." She cut off abruptly, those impassioned green irises widening as if she hadn't meant to admit that, and her lips pinched shut in dismay.

Story? Jasper's curiosity was pricked. His mouth quirked at the aghast expression she couldn't smother. "By all means, Sweetbriar, don't stop now when you have my rapt attention."

She scowled and waved a dismissive arm, though her

tense body betrayed her ambivalence. "Stories from the women at Lethe, of course."

"That's not what you meant, and we both know it," he said. "What kind of stories? Penny dreadfuls? Contributions to a lady's magazine perhaps? Or a circulating publication?" Her stifled inhalation made him grin. "I'm getting warmer! A novelette supplement in the newssheets? Or perhaps a yellowback? A serial?"

Her scowl grew. "You couldn't be further from the truth, Lord Jackass."

"You only call me that when you're hiding something," he said, watching her like a hawk. "Like being a secret author. Who is the publisher? Routledge? Chapman and Hall? H. Smith. Thomas Judge."

"How do you even know all those names? You're grasping at straws. Stop before you hurt yourself."

He smirked when she lifted her jaw. He'd spent enough time with her to recognize that tell-tale chin jut whenever she was prevaricating. "Keep your secrets, Prickles. You know I'll figure them out eventually."

If looks could kill, he would be floating down the Thames with a thousand cuts over his poor body. "Damn and blast, you are...bloody nauseating!"

"You love me," he said.

"On the contrary, the word you're looking for is *loathe* not love. Now, bugger off."

He only grinned as he followed her across the street. "Do you kiss your mother with that mouth? Or is that part of your saucy literary persona?"

"Worry about your own mouth, you lout. And no, *you* bring this side spectacularly out of me."

He chuckled. *Likewise.*

London had its share of writers, especially female ones, who hid their true identities. In the early part of the century, Mary Shelley and Jane Austen both penned novels anonymously, and the Brontë sisters wrote under male pseudonyms. Most gothic literature, even ones written by men, was under pen names or nameless.

Jasper, along with most of London, had read the enormously provocative novels of John Cleland and the Marquis de Sade as well as many other anonymous erotic titles. The thought of Briar penning a potentially salacious novel made his growing arousal sharpen.

Years ago, Jasper had overheard whispered chatter of a secret writer in his sister's tight group of friends, though he'd never seen any obvious proof of the fact. He'd assumed it to be a passing hobby of one of the girls, but this sounded... bigger than a mere pastime. *Did* she write and publish racy stories inspiring female pleasure?

By a simple process of elimination, it wouldn't surprise him if it *were* Briar.

His sister preferred numbers to words, Marsden's marchioness was a fashion designer, the Duchess of Montcroix was a ballerina, and the Duchess of Vale was obsessed with her animal shelters. Briar, however, was unapologetically vocal in her opinions, especially when it came to women's rights and bodily autonomy, and in her spare time, she adored reading. Sensation fiction, particularly, and especially of the gothic and romantic variety.

Christ, *was* the little virago a secret erotic novelist?

Given their collaborative efforts at Lethe, the social and gambling club in West London he owned, he wasn't surprised in the least by her earlier boasts that she would be privy to scandalous gossip in the upper rooms—some of the women they rescued who chose to become employed at the establishment weren't shy about their former professions as courtesans.

As Briar herself had emphatically stated to him more than once, work of a sexual or sensual nature was *work*, and women's bodies belonged to the women who fed, cared for, and nourished them. Not a man.

Jasper didn't disagree—in his mind, a woman could do what she wanted with her own person, provided it was her decision and not someone else's. Too bad most of their society didn't think the same. However, despite the social restrictions placed on women in general, Jasper deeply admired what Briar was doing at Lethe. An avid supporter of women's rights, she fought fiercely for the disadvantaged and downtrodden any chance she got.

When she'd first approached him with the audacious idea of hiring the women she saved from destitution by offering them jobs and paying them fair wages at his club, he'd laughed in her face. He wasn't running a brothel—it was a boxing and social club. But in the end, Briar had worn him down with her unassailable logic: give her a chance and *she* would garnish their wages out of her own pin money.

An entire year later and Jasper had an army of cooks, maids, performers, clerks, messengers, and even an on-site team of seamstresses working at Lethe. And true to her word, Briar had compensated them out of her own funds. Where she had the substantial income to do so, Jasper hadn't known. He'd assumed she had received them from her father.

But perhaps her writing endeavors had done well for her.

Damn, what he wouldn't do to get his hands on one of those stories...or at least find out where she published and under what name. He would bet anything that it was a nom de plume. Society would shred her alive if she were open about her identity as an author.

Were her erotic publications the source of all her so-called sensual knowledge? She wouldn't deign to respond if he asked, Jasper knew. She was an impenetrable vault when she wanted to be. No, getting answers from Briar meant goading her into responding.

"So, do you have proof of this supposedly carnal knowledge?" he drawled.

Her eyes launched daggers in his direction as Jasper folded his arms and leaned against the carriage door, blocking it from being opened. Luckily, her coachman, who was always armed, knew him well. Olsen had been privy to several of their explosive exchanges and understood when to look the other way.

"Proof?" Oh, the scathing vitriol in that one word had his cock rock-hard. Perhaps he was a glutton for punishment... her brand of punishment. A scandalized but amused gaze slid slowly down his torso as she took a step closer instead of pulling away, bridging the small gap between them. "Do you mean to shock me, my lord? Or perhaps you only intend to provoke with such an unseemly demand. Do you truly wish for a demonstration of my understanding of connubial matters?"

Jasper should have recognized that dangerous glint in her eyes—the one that forewarned she was going to do something unexpected and usually controversial—but he was too hypnotized by the suddenly sultry tenor of her voice. It sounded like thickened honey, velvet over whetted steel. Light fingertips danced up his chest, leaving spots of fire in their wake, and suddenly, he wished he could take back the challenge he'd issued.

This was a terrible fucking idea.

"Bri—"

A torrid gaze full of promise peered up through that thick fringe of lashes as her fingers wound into the hair over his collar, suffocating the second part of her name when she tugged him down, so her breath feathered over his chin. "Should I whisper it in your ear then, my lord? Describe what it feels like when undressed bodies collide in a feverish explosion of luscious heat and whispered nothings. When a man's hard phallus slides home into a glistening sheath that's so welcoming and silky and *wet*, there's no end or beginning to where they've joined, only the sweetest of friction, punctuated by indelicate moans of rapture."

"Christ, Briar—" he choked, his cock swelling to full mast without any provocation but the lush decadence of her words. Good God, were his fucking ears on fire? Was the *rest* of him? He could have sworn the minx had licked his lobe there at the end.

He wrenched at his cravat, sweat beading over his skin.

"What's the matter, Lord Lushing? Are my words bothering you? A bit hot under the collar?" Her melting gaze hardened to ice as her fingers curled into the strands at his nape and yanked hard. "Well, you should bloody know better than to challenge me, you bottle-headed, maggot-pated, jingle brains!" She stomped on his instep for good measure.

"Ouch!" he groaned and rubbed his sore scalp, even as his excruciatingly swollen groin *ached* for more. He hoped she wouldn't look down. In fact, he was surprised his cock wasn't punching through the obscenely tented fabric. A bit of goading was one thing; sporting an enormous erection when she'd practically wiped the floor with him with her visceral imaginings, was another. "What the hell was that for?"

"That's for being a prick!" She glared, lurching forward, her knee in a much too precarious position, and Jasper covered his distended, vulnerable crotch with both hands. Her cheeks flared brighter as her hands fisted, a pulse hammering in her neck.

"*You* made the boast," he shot back and reached up to his smarting nape. Fuck, she had ripped out a good handful of his hair. "Therefore, the burden of proof was on you, was it not?"

"You were being vulgar, and you know it."

He stared pointedly at her gentlemen's garb and arched his brows with a mocking grin. "We're not in a London drawing room. In fact, we are in a very *vulgar* part of the city. You cannot have your cake *and* eat your cake."

"You are unendurable!"

Chuckling, Jasper reared back when she bared her teeth and *growled* at him. The question bubbled to his lips with no thought to his personal safety as she shoved him rudely out of the way and climbed into her coach. "Tell me, Poison Ivy, was that from one of the special stories that we are pretending not to talk about?"

Briar went still and then shook her head, muttering a slew of smothered curses.

"Olsen, go," she ordered the coachman with a rap to the roof, her gorgeous face flushed. "Before I commit murder right here in the street."

"Such violence for someone so tiny," Jasper teased, holding the coach door open with one palm. Thankfully, Olsen did not drive off as directed; the dependable coachman was much too familiar with this song and dance.

Her stare melted into a glower as she rose and braced on the other side of the door, the height of the coach allowing her to meet him eye-to-eye. "Devil take it, Lushing, do you practice daily to be this aggravating?"

"Only for you," Jasper said, as she rammed his hand away with surprising strength and slammed the door. "Good thing you idolize me."

"You must be confused," she said, glaring at him through the small open window. "Because I emphatically, unequivocally, and will *forever* despise the air you breathe!"

"Stop lying to yourself, Prickles," he teased in a sing-song voice loudly, knowing it would irritate the spit out of her. Sure enough, the sound of her snarl was music to his ears.

"Argh, go...go sit on a pile of...knitting needles!"

He laughed. "That's oddly specific, Sweetbriar."

Loud grumbling and thumping sounds reached him when a small ankle boot came flying out of the window right at his head, and he dodged it, even as she continued fuming. Retrieving the shoe, he nodded to Olsen, who rolled his eyes at their antics as the carriage finally pulled away.

"Give me back my boot, you princock!" Briar bellowed.

Wagging a single finger, Jasper shook his head. "He that finds, keeps, and he that loses weeps."

"You are the worst!"

"I'm not the one throwing footwear out of carriages like an uncivilized ruffian."

Holding the small black-and-tan leather boot with its delicate button hooks and embroidered edging, he half expected its pair to come hurtling out of the coach window as well. But to his everlasting disappointment, it did not.

His mouth quirked. There was always tomorrow.

CHAPTER THREE

"You look quite well, my dear," Preston said, his pale blue eyes glinting in the light of the gas lamps as they stood on the edge of the ballroom, where they had been for the last hour at least, standing like statues. "That color suits you."

"Thank you, my lord." Briar smiled demurely at his lackluster compliment. The jejune pastel-pink colored gown wasn't one of her favorites, but she knew he liked it. Probably because she resembled a fresh-faced debutante just out of the schoolroom.

The bodice went higher than was fashionable, past her collarbones and nearly halfway up her throat, and the fitted sleeves felt like arm-length manacles. Each of the cascading layers of the skirt was embroidered with pink roses and ribbons. It wasn't a *terrible* dress; it just wasn't her style. Her preference ran to bold colors—lustrous golds, emerald greens, and sapphire blues. Like the dark-blue eyes of a certain gentleman when they caught the light just right.

No, no, no.

Lushing's eyes were nothing of note. Blue was an ordinary color. Prosaic, almost. Except when they were gleaming with humor and teasing wickedness, and their bottomless depths would tempt any maiden into carnal acts of depravity.

She would know...

Briar had pretended to be aggravated in Seven Dials the other evening, but in truth, their impassioned, indecent, and categorically invigorating interlude had been gratifying. So much so that she'd lost a boot over it. A smile tugged at her lips. *Not a single regret...*

She loved that he didn't care about the unruly words that came out of her mouth, or the fact that she'd been dressed in men's clothing, or even that she'd been alone, scaring the living daylights out of two ruffians. Unlike other gentlemen, Lushing trusted that she was capable of handling herself. That she wasn't some simpering, swooning damsel to be rescued at every turn.

Though she secretly adored that he was so gallantly protective, while not undermining her autonomy. In truth, when she *didn't* run into him, it felt like something was wrong. Her thoughts faltered. When had she started hoping to see him on her jaunts through the city streets? Their rapport was so mercurial: hot, one minute, cold the next. And yet, she relished it.

Though that was neither here nor there since according to his sister, the rogue was finally ready to take himself off the marriage mart by proposing to Lady Penelope. He wouldn't be dogging her footsteps while she gallivanted about the West End playing soldier of the bodyguard anymore...but focusing on his future bride. As he should be. Briar ignored the odd, sharpened spike behind her ribcage.

Vesper had let slip that this ball was likely when her brother was going to ask the lady for her hand in marriage. The news had hit Briar strangely, but there was no way that she was going to pick apart why she felt at sixes and sevens. Lushing was at the very least a friend, and sometimes, not even that. He was her best friend's brother. He was her reluctant business partner. And most days, he was her archenemy. Whether either of them tied the knot had no bearing on their professional arrangement.

Still, something deep inside ached with a peculiar feeling of loss. Not that the infuriatingly handsome earl had ever been Briar's to lose.

Penelope was lovely, if one liked biddable, dainty, milk-and-water ladies, and the two of them made an excellent match. As if they'd been summoned by her thoughts, the majordomo announced their names. A vicious swarm of wasps formed in her belly when she peered up at the happy couple entering the ballroom at the top of the stairs. Her throat tightened.

Lushing looked dapper and entirely too attractive. Penelope was a beautiful girl with glossy blond hair and rosy skin —the perfect foil to a gentleman like the tall, dazzling earl beside her. She would undoubtedly give him a handful of starched, immaculately behaved, cherubic heirs. Mirth bubbled in Briar's chest. Whereas, if she and Lushing ever had the misfortune to procreate, their spawn would be wild and disorderly with rumpled grass-stained clothing. The image of curly redheads with burnished gold-brown skin and gap-toothed smiles appeared before she could curb her thoughts.

Deuce it, why on earth was she imagining children with *him*?

If anything, she should be thinking of heirs with Preston.

Of course she would never admit it to Lushing, but the thought of bedding the viscount *was* off-putting. Their few perfunctory pecks had inspired little desire within her. It was not the kind of omen she wanted for the marriage bed. Deep down, Briar craved what the girls at Lethe talked about in hushed voices—lust, and hunger, and breathless cataclysms. She wanted to be transported, to have her body be played like a fiddle...much like the heroine in her stories.

Despite what she'd boasted to Lushing, she had no *empirical* evidence of copulation, but she knew about passion...and the viscount was the opposite of a passionate man. Coitus to him would be cursory. No doubt she *would* be expected to lie there and think of England. A pulse of despondency rippled in her chest.

You chose this, she reminded herself. *For good reason.*

Well, at least she could enjoy her last few weeks of the season. Her feet tapped to the music as the country reel that had started earlier grew more boisterous. She'd give her left arm to join the dancers. Anything was better than standing in silence like a mute marionette next to a man who seemed to begrudge anything fun.

"Do stop fidgeting," came the brisk, low-pitched command.

"It's music, my lord," she blurted without thinking, peering up at her fiancé through her lashes. "Do you not enjoy the beat?"

She knew he wasn't one for dancing—the viscount believed such pastimes, especially the waltz, were immoral and paved the way for sin. Briar suppressed her eyeroll. Heaven forbid a man and a woman hold each other twelve inches apart dancing on a public dance floor. Cue the scandalmongers! As her friend Nève, the Duchess of Montcroix, would say in a tone brimming with French sarcasm, quelle horreur!

"It's uncouth," he said. "The future wife of a peer should stand quietly and demurely, head bowed, and hands clasped like a virtuous and devout lady, not tapping her feet like an ill-mannered simpleton."

Briar blinked. *Head bowed and hands clasped...at a ball?*

"Why? We're not in a chapel," she replied before she could stop herself.

That retort earned her a sharp stare, his disapproval obvious. "You are to be *my* wife and will conduct yourself as *I* see fit."

She sucked in a breath to stop a scathing retort from leaving her lips. Spending time with Lushing had evidently made her tongue looser than usual, not that she was blaming him. She wasn't. Briar could say the most ribald thing, and Lushing would never reprimand her or treat her like a child. The scoundrel did not give a whit for respectability. But Preston wasn't the earl. Propriety was his entire personality.

Briar soothed her spark of temper. "Of course, my lord. Although in my defense, this is a ball, and people are expected to dance. I'll stop fidgeting. You're right, it is an unbecoming habit."

He glanced down the length of his nose at her, pale gaze assessing her sincerity before he gave a decisive nod. "In our marriage, I expect you to live up to your father's station,

Lady Briar. You are the daughter of a peer and will be the wife of one." His mouth pursed, and Briar swallowed her sass —he'd been a viscount for all of five minutes. She nodded demurely. "And if you expect me to keep your home in Bath, you will abide by my wishes. Obedience and piety are all I require." His hand gripped her chin in an unbreakable hold that pinched, though outwardly, Briar knew it would appear to be a tender caress. She forced her face to remain placid, despite the cruel fingers pressing into her jaw. "For your father's sake."

Ice slithered over her heart. Clearly, Preston meant the agreement he and her papa had made as part of the suit— her hand in marriage and an understanding that her childhood home in Bath would never be sold as long as they remained married. It was not an entailed property but would be part of her dowry.

Her father wanted Briar to be settled, especially because after his death, the earldom would return to the crown without any male heirs. Since her papa was an only child of an only child, without any male relatives, his title would become extinct. Her half-brothers could not inherit since they were not related by blood. And bloodlines in the British laws of primogeniture were a devil of a thing. The Earl of Rubens would be no more, and the entailed estate in Essex would revert to the crown.

It was absurd that the English laws meant that women could not inherit their family's property or titles. In Scotland, female heirs could inherit both! Some Scottish peerages had remainders allowing inheritance through women, either directly or through heirs. Effie's Scottish mother-in-law had been a peeress in her own right, before her marriage to the

Duke of Vale's father. She still lived in the Highlands on her own ancestral lands.

Briar sniffed. At least with this marriage, even though the property would not be *hers* or in her name, she could keep the home in Bath that was full of memories of her happy upbringing and most of her childhood. Her throat worked at the threat Preston held over her head. Would he sell it if she didn't behave? If she did not conduct herself accordingly? The thought grated.

"Of course, my lord," she managed politely when he released her jaw. She hoped it wouldn't bruise, but perhaps it was a blessing that her light brown skin hid a lot more than a fairer complexion would. Preston was fond of furtive pinching whenever he was displeased, as the backs of her arms, currently hidden by long gloves, could attest.

The pinches were of little consequence. They did not happen often, unless she incited him for some mundane reason. Once they were married, she would be sure to stay out of his reach...and his petulant, self-righteous temper. For now, she would endure. Weaving her fingers together in front of her, Briar watched enviously as the dancers whirled by in a rousing polka.

Those were glorious fun, especially in the company of her friends.

Her feet itched to join them, but a dance or two was a fair sacrifice for a husband who would ultimately leave her to her own devices. At least, that was the plan. It required some finesse on her part to convince Preston that she was demure enough to satisfy his expectations of a wife and yet be insipid enough for him to ignore...so he would seek out a mistress for companionship. She was in the minority, Briar knew.

None of her fierce friends would ever tolerate if their husbands wandered. Not that those men *would*...they were all stupidly, irrevocably in love with their wives. And her friends deserved every happiness.

Envy tugged at her, but a union like theirs wasn't in her future. Briar didn't need love...she needed autonomy and space to fulfill her true calling. The right husband would ensure that. She had income from her stories to help other women. She had a place at Lethe. She would continue her work with the suffragettes, fighting for women's rights. She would be *fulfilled*.

She could handle Preston and a few peeved pinches.

If she made herself invisible, he'd lose interest in her.

Still, Briar exhaled a soundless sigh when her best friends whirled by with their partners. Nève and the stoic Montcroix, Laila and her smitten marquess, Vesper and the boy-next-door she'd loved practically forever, and lastly, Effie and her devoted Scottish duke who was once called the worst duke in London by the *Times*. If Briar ever met a person who looked at her the way Vale looked at Effie, she wouldn't give a hoot what the newssheets wrote.

A redheaded rogue with a wicked smirk pranced over her vision. Briar snorted. Lushing didn't look at her like that; he looked at her with utter exasperation. Like he wanted nothing more than to put her over his knee...

She went breathless. *No, Briar, do* not *go there.*

Swallowing hard, she tugged at her collar but dropped her hand at a censorious noise from Preston. She bit her lip, reminding herself that she had to get into his good graces.

Her mind, though, kept wandering. Was Lushing's engagement one of convenience like hers would be? Did he even *like* Penelope? She would wager that the cocky libertine wouldn't know true love if it bit him in the arse, but then again, he was about to propose, so maybe that had changed. Penelope was the season's diamond, and there wasn't a soul alive who wasn't won over by Lushing. Despite their constant bickering, he was *likable*.

And deep down under all that self-aggrandizing, he was kind.

When he followed her into seedier areas of London, he was being considerate. Like a friend or brother would. She would know—she had four of them, and eluding their constant hovering had become a study in strategy and subterfuge. Her elder brothers weren't so bad, given the substantial age differences between them, but the youngest —a trained police inspector—was harder to trick. She adored Levi, ten years her senior, but he was no fool.

That was why he'd taught her how to defend herself.

The strains of a quadrille started, and Briar bit back another sigh as her stolid companion made no move to ask her to dance. Not that she expected him to, but a girl could hope. Surely a modest quadrille would be acceptable. She sent him an imploring gaze, which he ignored. Instead, he marched away to converse with another guest, leaving her alone to hold up a pillar like a sad, rejected wallflower.

"Enjoying the ball, Sweetbriar?" a deep voice drawled from behind her.

Briar hid her smile and ignored the warm rush in her chest. "I don't think your future bride will appreciate you calling another woman by a nickname, Lord Lushing."

He propped a shoulder onto the nearest pillar. "Future bride? What have you heard?" He chuckled when she rolled her eyes. "Or rather, what has my loose-lipped sister told you?"

"My lips are perfectly tight, I'll have you know," Vesper said, appearing with the Duke of Greydon, her eyes bright. "Ask my darling husband."

"Vesper!" Effie chided with a horrified giggle as she too arrived on the arm of her Scottish spouse. It was as though they'd been waiting for Preston to leave, or perhaps the timing of the end of the set was simply coincidence. Briar didn't think so, however. Preston had an air of moral superiority that she knew her friends disliked. "Don't mind your sister, Lushing, she's utterly foxed," Effie said.

"It's the truth, isn't it, Aspen my love?" Vesper crooned to her duke. "You always say my mouth is like my—"

With a choked sound, Greydon covered her lips with his palm. He had his hands full with his vivacious, outspoken wife whom he adored with every bone in his body. *Every* bone, as Vesper had boasted to the Hellfire Kitties more than once. God love her, but her tongue was even worse than Briar's, and Briar spent her days with countless courtesans.

"Where are Nève and Laila?" Briar asked, taking pity on the duke and redirecting the conversation before Vesper started spilling *all* their private bedroom secrets.

Effie pointed over her shoulder. "Getting refreshments or canoodling in a corner. We are never quite sure which. Canoodling, I suspect, since they have vanished quite suspiciously."

"No one told *me* canoodling was an option," the Duke of Vale rumbled, his eyes sparkling as Effie laid her head on his arm with a flirty wink. Love had transformed dear Effie, too. She was glowing with the confidence of a well-loved woman, and she no longer stayed out of the public eye like an oddity who didn't belong. No, she celebrated her eccentricities. Her besotted mountain of a Scot would have had something to do with that.

"Good things come to those who wait, Your Grace," Effie teased, but she didn't protest as her duke tugged her toward the balcony, and she waved a half-hearted goodbye to them.

Briar's chest squeezed. Her friends were all deliriously happy, and she felt...a curious melancholy. Preston already hated them. He'd previously made comments that they were dangerous women with dangerous ideas. Briar bit back a snort. Little did he know that the Hellfire Kitties made *danger* look like an afternoon stroll in the park.

"Where's your viscount?" Vesper asked, the title emerging like something sour. Her best friend thought she was settling, and while it wasn't untrue, Vesper didn't know that there were other things of importance at play. Like saving the only home she'd ever known. Like continuing her work with the women at Lethe. Like marrying a man who would not get in her way.

She surveyed the ballroom and saw Preston standing near Penelope. "Over there talking to some people, including your future sister-in-law." Briar glanced at the earl, who, in typical Lushing fashion, wore an amused expression that gave no hint of his true feelings. "Though your brother seems to be prevaricating as usual."

Vesper leaned in with a scowl that she didn't care to hide from anyone and made a gagging noise. "That chit is bloody awful. A doormat has more personality than she does. I have no idea why my idiot brother is so fixated on ruining his life with someone so lackluster and uninspiringly unoriginal that she makes seaweed scrapbooking seem like fun!"

Briar's eyes rounded while Lushing arched an auburn brow at his sister's exceptionally creative rant. "You got one thing correct, sister dear. It's *my* life to ruin as I see fit with whomever I choose."

"But why her?" Vesper whined and wrinkled her pert nose. "She's such a...stick-in-the-mud. Briar, tell him!"

Briar huffed and shook her head. "Oh, no. Don't involve me in your sibling squabbles. Besides, I happen to think that seaweed crafting is quite an interesting pastime, though arguably, it's not for everyone. Margaret Gatty published quite an extensive collection, I believe."

"Oh, a pox on seaweeding!" With a deepening sulk, Vesper pouted, gaze vacillating between them. "You two should marry. Why won't you? Everyone knows you're perfect for each other, even if you don't see it because you're both stubborn and mutton-brained. In fact, you should go dance and discuss this. I deserve a wonderful sister-in-law! I deserve a Hellfire Kitty sister! Don't let Viscount Sackless ruin our chance at happiness."

Briar burst into cackles at the insulting nickname as Greydon collected his fervid wife and drew her into his arms. "Not everything is about you, my love," he said with an apologetic look in their direction. "Come on, Viper, let's get you some water."

The silence stretched as the Duke of Greydon guided his protesting but quite inebriated duchess away. It was Vesper's first ball after the birth of her daughter, Audra, who had arrived rather early but was thriving now, thank goodness. It had been a tough few months for them, but mercifully, they had just turned a corner, which was why the couple was out tonight. They deserved the respite. No wonder her friend was in her cups.

"Sackless?" Lushing murmured, not even hiding the glee in his tone when they stood alone once more.

Briar swallowed her snort. "Don't you start."

"I wasn't."

She glared. "You *were*. You simply cannot help yourself."

"You're right," he admitted. "Not when teasing you and collecting randomly thrown shoes have now become my life's mission."

A laugh broke from her, making those blue eyes of his light with a burst of true pleasure. Briar blinked, words suddenly evading her. His eyes were beautiful, but in that singular moment, crinkled at the corners and sparkling with joy, they shone. She cleared her throat. "I want that boot back, by the way."

"What will you give me for it?"

"My gratitude."

He canted his head. "Perhaps we should dance like my sister suggested and discuss terms of surrender."

"For a *boot*?" she asked incredulously.

Flames lit in his eyes. "Or in general."

Briar inhaled sharply, a lick of heat curling up her spine as her knees went stupidly weak beneath her skirts. She must have misheard him. Of course, he didn't mean *her* surrender, even though that was exactly how it sounded. Why did the thought of ceding control leave her so breathless?

"Vesper's foxed," she said, striving for equanimity. "I

wouldn't put much stock in her demands. And she probably won't remember any of this anyway."

"Afraid, Prickles?" he taunted.

Goodness, when did being called Prickles start making her feel warm inside? She *hated* the sobriquet. Her breath hitched in her throat as that singular gaze roved over her features, and she nearly drowned in that ocean-blue, unreadable stare. Her chest constricted with that strange ache again. Their normal testy push-and-pull had lost its sharpened edge.

Cheeks warming, she ducked her head. "Hardly."

"Then dance with me."

The soft request felt...weighted, as if something momentous were shifting between them. Or perhaps that was only her, being mesmerized by a pair of pretty eyes and imagining scenarios that did not exist. Despite their tetchy relationship, Briar did care about him. He'd been a part of her life for so long that he was a permanent fixture.

Was that why seeing him moving on with someone else hurt in a way she couldn't parse? Had he felt the same when she'd accepted Preston's suit?

Lushing had always been the perpetual bachelor, never settling down with any one woman. Until now...until *she* had become engaged.

Briar frowned. Was *that* why? The timing did seem peculiar, but perhaps she was reading into things. Perhaps it was entirely accidental. She glanced over to where Preston was still occupied in deep conversation, his expression somber and grim. Her fingers flitted up to her jaw, where her face was still tender. A surge of despair filled her, followed by anger.

She wasn't married *yet*.

"You know what, Lushing? Let's dance. In fact, I'd be delighted to."

Briar pulled her cloak tighter around her neck as an unseasonably cold wind blew through the streets of Piccadilly. The pamphlets in her hand were nearly distributed. It was a risk for her as a peeress to be handing out such contentious information so publicly, but they were short-handed, and her friend, Millicent Fawcett, the founder of the London National Society for Women's Suffrage, had asked her a personal favor.

The latest pamphlet had been printed out of necessity to combat the recent demeaning article in the *Times*. Briar could recall the scathing editorial almost verbatim.

No woman has yet pretended to be on a level with men in physical strength. They have at present the privileges and the protection of the weak. Let them undertake to defend themselves, and they must be content with the bare rights they can enforce. Instead of gaining any additional rights, they would risk some of the rights they possess; and they would inevitably lose the peculiar influence which is now derived from their very subordination.

Just thinking about the inherent misogyny made Briar boil. *The weak, her fractious arse!* It was a slap in the face, considering the wide distribution of the newspaper, but it was also a rallying cry to everyone fighting for a woman's right to vote, including a steadfast handful of aristocrats. Briar was one of them.

Sadly, and perhaps ironically, the movement did not have

the support of the current *female* monarch who proclaimed their effort a mad, wicked folly and had apparently called for both Viscountess Amberley and Briar to get a good whipping.

Apart from the personal attack toward them, the queen's reaction had been disheartening to say the least, setting them back leaps in their work toward any equality of the sexes. Their small but fierce group fought against the patriarchy at every turn, only to be undermined by a woman in a unique position of power who should have been their strongest advocate.

It was entirely frustrating.

Briar scowled. Despite what many thought, women weren't meant to be subordinate to men. They had their own capable minds and deserved governance over their own minds and bodies. A woman's place was in some part the home, true, but she should be given the *choice* in what she wanted in addition to that. Their existence was by nature political. Claiming politics was *unfeminine* was an excuse to pigeonhole women into accepting the lot that was decided for them by someone else.

When Millicent had asked for help, Briar had readily agreed. She'd already planned to visit her printer that morning to discuss the latest circulating copy of her very secret but lucrative publication: *Lady Ivy Thorn, Or A Study in Secrets*, a fictional heiress turned courtesan who narrated her sexual explorations. It wasn't any hardship to hand out the pamphlets afterward.

No hardship...unless Briar was seen by someone she knew, which was not likely. Certainly not at this early hour of the morning. Everyone in the pampered *ton* was still abed.

A twinge of discomfort ran through her at the thought of her fiancé. Preston would not approve of this. She grimaced and shook her head. What the viscount didn't know wouldn't hurt him.

This, Lethe, *and* her writing...

Her thoughts turned back to the latest installment of her own work that had taken London by storm for the past few years. Thanks to the encouragement of the Hellfire Kitties, and certainly to Vesper who had named Briar the resident rhyparographer—scribe of sordid things—she'd taken the steps to publish under a pen name years ago when Laila had married Marsden. It had been self-funded with her pin money at first until the income had started flowing in.

To the surprise of no one, at least in her progressive circles, women were salivating over the racy stories that challenged the status quo and put female pleasure at the forefront. They were much too accustomed to being silent, inert receptacles for impregnation and being taught to be ashamed instead of seeking satisfaction for their own sensual desires.

Thanks to Lady Ivy Thorn, Englishwomen were being armed with a wealth of sexual knowledge one scandalous, consensual story at a time. Lady Ivy didn't shy away from her needs or taking what she wanted when she wanted. The latest issue had been Briar's wickedest yet.

None of the stories were from actual experience, but a collage of ideas cobbled together from tales told by the women who worked at Lethe in addition to Briar's meticulous research across the globe, as well as her own secret fantasies...which more often than not featured a man with tousled auburn hair, the tongue of a serpent, and the charm of the devil.

It wasn't Lushing.

It was simply a fluke that her fictional lovers were tall and broad-shouldered with eyes resembling the ocean at twilight and a pair of sinful lips that would put the most talented of Parisian courtesans to shame.

In truth, Lushing *had* been a convenient, harmless fixation at first. Until he opened his mouth.

Admittedly, Briar had been infatuated with her best friend's brother for years, but when that infatuation had evolved into mutual loathing—started by *him*—her fascination with the man had grown fangs and turned into a monster.

She reviled him...and yet, she desired him.

Thereafter, her most intimate fantasies had become utterly depraved...things that no modest lady could ever confess for fear of accusations of hysteria and confinement in an asylum. Dreams of being commanded and praised, even degraded to some degree. She was what Preston would decidedly call a horny abomination, not that he or any of her friends, for that matter, knew how far her wantonness descended.

She wanted to be on her knees, being told when to breathe, choking on...

Bloody hell.

Briar flushed, even with the bite of the cold wind, her entire body heating. Perhaps of all the Hellfire Kitties, Effie had an inkling of some shared erotic interests, though she wasn't a woman to judge or share her private opinions on sensual matters. Effie was a quiet contradiction. She had always been the most reserved one in their group, and yet, she was the one who advocated heavily for self-pleasure and had pursued lessons in carnality with her duke.

Then again, there was an adage about still waters running deep for a reason.

Too bad your own waters runneth over in every direction.

Briar chuckled and bit her lip.

This was why Viscount Sackley would be good for her. Beyond the material gains of the Bath estate and not being particularly attracted to her as far as she could discern, he was sedate and reserved. Pious and proper. He would not incite the feral, sensual creature that hummed beneath her skin and was desperate for escape. In fact, she hoped he might calm it, even suppress it.

Contrary to what Vesper thought, the viscount *was* the perfect husband for her, especially considering her own impetuous nature, and a man like Lushing—even imaginary —would only enflame proclivities better left buried.

For everyone's sake.

With a sigh, Briar handed out the last of the pamphlets to a passerby without looking up and froze when the person's palm closed over hers in a punishing, pinching grip.

"I beg your pardon—" she spluttered, and then then her voice trailed off as her eyes collided with an irate face...one she *never* expected to see, even though she'd *just* been thinking of him.

"I had hoped the disturbing news I received this early morning would not be true," the enraged viscount snapped, his voice a whip of displeasure. "That you were not here, conducting yourself with such impropriety unbecoming of a lady."

Briar's stomach dropped. "My lord, wait. I can explain—"

Preston lifted the pamphlet in disgust and crumpled it in his fist. "But after that performance with that degenerate rake the other night, I should not be surprised. I forbade you to make a spectacle of yourself, and you still chose to make a *fool* out of me."

Goodness, was he talking about the *quadrille*? She and Lushing had barely touched, though the undercurrent she'd felt between them hadn't dissipated the entire evening. The strange tension had been present, but she hadn't dwelled on it, chalking it up to some kind of nostalgic yearning at their diverging paths. Had others like the viscount noticed something untoward?

"Preston, please. The earl is an acquaintance, nothing more. I..."

His mouth curled into an ugly sneer as he cut her off. "In the future, should our paths cross, you will address me as Viscount Sackley, Lady Briar, or perhaps not at all, which would be vastly preferable. I should not like to surround myself with such...vulgarity."

Those pale eyes glimmered with rancor, and beneath the judgment, there was something else she couldn't quite name. Something darkly sentientous that made her shiver, her gut sparking with instinctive alarm. "What are you saying?" she asked.

"I must withdraw my suit."

"My lord—"

But the viscount was already walking away.

Trembling, she watched in horror as all her carefully laid plans vanished with the wind.

CHAPTER FOUR

"Brother!" Vesper shrieked, making both Greydon and their father wince where they sat on the other side of the table on the outdoor patio during a late Saturday breakfast.

Jasper's brows rose as his sister barreled toward them with some single-minded purpose. The baby in her arms gave a loud wail, the hapless nurse following in their wake. Vesper held crumpled newssheets in her free hand, waving them with a giddy fervor that made his eyes narrow. Her eyes held an exhilarated glint he hadn't seen in a while.

Oh, no. He *knew* that look. It was her *matchmaking* look.

He'd only escaped from her attempts to match him with several heiresses in the *ton* because he'd put his foot down years ago. But clearly that understanding was at an end.

This was about Penelope, he surmised. Ever since the ball, Vesper had gotten a bee in her bonnet that it was up to her to set him on the right course for a wife. That being anyone but the woman he'd selected.

"I think you meant *husband*, not brother," he said, pointing obsequiously at his brother-in-law. "He's the one you should seek out on all matters, including whatever tomfooleries you've concocted in that head of yours."

Ignoring him, she shoved the newssheets onto the table and jammed her finger toward a small, printed section on the left side. "Here is your chance to make things right. This is kismet. *Fate*. Now you only need to do something about it." Her entire body fairly vibrated with zeal. "And if you do not follow through with this, I shall make it my personal goal to make your life a living hell—*that* I promise you. Stop staring at me like a simpleton and read, for the love of everything holy!"

Blinking at the unexpected diatribe, Jasper grasped the newspaper and skimmed the announcement in the *Times* of the engagement of one Viscount Sackley to Lady Penelope Adler.

Jasper read it again, curiously feeling nothing at the latter name...the woman *he* had been dutifully courting for the past few weeks. Shouldn't he feel upset? Or angry? This was almost as bad as being jilted at the altar, especially when their courtship had been so public.

Everyone expected them to marry.

But no, all he felt was mild surprise, and then a shocking, *perilous* sense of relief. Had Briar cried off her engagement to the viscount?

"Has she said anything to you?" he asked his sister, currently soothing her grumpy daughter, who had been rudely awakened by her mama's antics.

Audra was the perfect mix of both her parents and adored by everyone. A smile feathered over his lips at the infant's owlish hoots when Vesper kissed her downy fore-head—the babe was beautiful and growing plumper every single day after an uncertain, frightening start. Jasper could not remember loving being a doting uncle more. Those little hoots could melt the hardest heart.

Vesper shook her head. "Trust me, it's as much a surprise to me as it is to you or anyone. Though I must say those two moist dishrags are better suited to each other. Viscount Sackless would have made our Briar miserable. And we all know that Penelope has the personality of a doornail." She made a face. "No offense."

Jasper took a sip of his coffee, hoping the benign action would calm his suddenly thundering pulse. "None taken. But this doesn't mean that Lady Briar wants *me* to court her. She doesn't even think of me in that way, no matter what your inventive little mind says or how much you desire her as a sister-in-law. You know very well that we are like oil and water, and never the twain shall mix."

"Hate and love are the two sides of the same coin," Vesper said sagely.

"I don't hate her," he murmured.

Her gaze sharpened and then narrowed with resolve. "And don't think I'm oblivious to the fact that she visits Lethe far more often than is proper. She's much too secretive about the goings-on there, when in truth, she should not have a membership as an unmarried lady. Her reputation would be in jeopardy."

Knowing his sister's talent to filch information from anywhere, Jasper sealed his lips. While he supported Briar's commendable efforts to help downtrodden women, it was not his place to divulge her private business. If she chose to reveal her charitable efforts to her friends, that was her choice. He pasted a blank mask on his face. "I have no idea what you're talking about. While we do welcome selective female members at Lethe, I do not know if she's a member or not."

"You know every person who has a membership, Jasper! It's your club!" If his sister's voice rose any further, it would crack crystal. Unsurprisingly, the babe in her arms startled and started to whimper again. "Now look at what you made me do," she groused as Greydon rose to scoop the fussing baby from her and soothe the infant against his shoulder.

Jasper squashed any reply after a sidelong glance from Greydon and a slight shake of his head. There was no reasoning with his sibling when she was in one of her moods. The display of mania and melancholy, according to their doctor—a revolutionary female doctor named Elizabeth Garrett—was common in some women weeks, months, and even years after giving birth. Given the trauma and despair that she'd endured after the arrival of Audra, they were all a little more careful with Vesper.

On top of her unique cognition, it had to be managed very carefully, as it was a cyclical disorder that could spiral quickly. Melancholia or puerperal insanity, as it was also called, was typically caused by mental distress. The treatment from Dr. Garrett included a healthy diet, rest, unlimited compassion, and plentiful help. She was adamantly against extremes like bloodletting or incarceration.

Thankfully, Greydon was a very devoted, hands-on father and worshipped the ground his wife walked on, for which both Jasper and their father were grateful.

Jasper exhaled and counted to ten in his head. "Yes, you're correct, but I am also well versed in Lethe's strict confidentiality rules," he replied in a mild tone. Finishing his coffee, he stood and cleared his throat, canting his head to both men. "Father, please excuse me. Greydon, good to see you. Sister, I shall take your advice under consideration." He meant to do no such thing, but placating Vesper was always the priority.

Mollified, she stared at him, uncertainty flashing in her blue eyes. "Good. Thank you, Jasper. I only want what's best for you, you know? I hope for you to find the kind of happiness as I have with Aspen. You deserve that."

It was on the tip of his tongue to respond that their kind of happiness was rare, and certainly not in the cards for him, but that wasn't what his well-intentioned sister wanted to hear.

"I know," he said, kissing her cheek. "Be sure to get some rest today."

As Jasper took his leave back to his own bachelor residence in St. James to gather his accounting ledgers before heading to Lethe, he wondered what had happened for Briar to break the engagement. From their conversation, she had seemed quite set on having the viscount for a husband. She thought he was *perfect*, after all.

As much as Jasper didn't like the man, he wasn't the one marrying him. The fact that the new engagement was to Lady Penelope had no real bearing on his opinions, though he did wonder at the appeal of such a man to someone like Penelope who had high hopes to make an excellent match that would please her mother. Heir to a dukedom, Jasper was considered one of the most eligible bachelors in London; the viscount was not.

That rubbed a bit.

Jasper frowned, his temper suddenly simmering. Who

did Sackley think he was? Surely the man would have known that the lady was spoken for. Wasn't there some sort of gentlemanly code of conduct when it came to courtship and coveting another man's future wife?

More importantly, should he be worried that Penelope had had such a late change of heart, considering she knew of his intentions? The official announcement hadn't happened after the ball—the timing had felt off for reasons Jasper couldn't explain—but that didn't mean it wasn't forthcoming. These announcements were mere formalities.

And in truth, he'd hoped to ask Penelope if this was truly what *she* wanted before any formal declaration was made. It was something Briar had said in Seven Dials about the duty of aristocratic heiresses, and the underlying despair in her tone had made him pause. But then, that damned ball had thrown him wildly off-balance. It'd felt like they were saying goodbye, and he couldn't bear that.

Caught in an odd funk that appeared out of nowhere, Jasper arrived at Lethe and went straight to his office, not noticing that someone was occupying the chair in front of his desk until he'd divested himself of his outer garments and sat down. He jumped at the sight of the woman who let out a low laugh at his disconcerted expression.

"Distracted, my lord?" she asked.

"Minthe, what are you doing here?" he asked the former courtesan turned bookkeeper. She was one of Briar's charges —a woman who'd been down on her luck and lost her position at a high-end brothel when she'd had to take care of a sick relative. Minthe had been hired as a server in the card rooms at Lethe, whereupon Jasper had discovered she had an uncommon talent with numbers. Within short order, he'd promoted her to assistant bookkeeper of the entire club without batting an eyelash. "I do need to go over some expenses with you, but were you waiting for me?"

"There's a problem," she said, her voice low.

He frowned. "What is it?"

"A message was delivered for Lady Briar." Minthe's face showed distress before it was smoothed away.

"What message?"

"Here," Minthe said, handing him the note that was written on plain parchment in blocky handwriting. "It wasn't sealed," she added hurriedly.

Jasper read aloud, "I know your secret. I have my eyes on you, little dove."

His breath stalled as he frowned, fingers balling into a fist at the subtle menace in the note, his body reacting as it always did whenever it came to Briar's safety. He didn't like that someone was watching her...and clearly wanted her to know it.

He glanced at Minthe. "Are you certain this was for Lady Briar? There's no name on this. Did the messenger say who gave it to him?"

Minthe exhaled with a small nod. "The boy who delivered it said her name clearly." She pinched her lips between her teeth, her expression betraying her tension and anger. "When I asked who it was from, he said a rich gent in a plain coach gave it to him."

"A rich gent? For it to be delivered *here*?" Jasper asked, brows crashing. "And not her address in Mayfair. That seems odd, no?"

"Yes," Minthe said. "It feels targeted."

Jasper cursed. "That it does. I don't like it."

"Do you think it's someone who wants to expose what she does at Lethe?" Minthe asked with a narrowed stare. "It can't be good for her reputation, mingling with the likes of us. And of course, being a partner in this." She waved an arm about the room. "It's not really the *done* thing for a lady of her station, is it?"

Jasper tilted his head, a frisson of worry coursing through him since Vesper had alluded to something similar barely an hour before. But besides that, how had Minthe guessed that he was in a silent partnership with Briar? No one knew of their agreement. "What do you mean?"

"I do the books, my lord. I can see who garnishes my wages, and I know you two have some business understanding. All I'm saying is that a lady of her rank, the daughter of an earl, isn't someone who should spend her time at a *gentleman's* social club." Her mouth pursed. "Word is flying around that Lethe is a safe haven for women like me, which is good, but you know how gossip is and how quickly anything *good* can turn to poison."

"Poison?" he echoed.

She shrugged. "The sanctimonious gossip rags are printing letters from concerned citizens that the club is nothing but a luxurious bawdy house, and if Lady Briar is associated with us, that could be used against her to tarnish her reputation."

Jasper was no stranger to being the center of attention with the newspapers—they always wanted something to write about, after all, and his many undertakings, including his investment in Lethe, had always been titillating fodder to them. Running a bawdy house was the least of his worries.

The implications for Briar, however, could be...dire, if word got out about her involvement.

A ruined reputation for a lady meant that her prospects for a good match would vanish. She would be shunned from polite society. People only needed the barest amount of conjecture to form an opinion that could very easily become misguided gospel. Jasper had seen it happen on many an occasion when an unscrupulous man's word was taken over a woman's and outright falsehoods became fact. Simply by default of one's sex. It was egregious and yet a repulsive reality in their world, one that needed to be changed. But change was slow.

Jasper studied the message again, wondering whether it had been written by a man or a woman. Not that it mattered —the malicious intent was the same. What did the writer of the note hope to accomplish? Was it a threat? Would there be more? He crumpled the note in his fist.

"Did you show this to Lady Briar?" he murmured.

Minthe shook her head. "She's not here, or I would have, but I also wanted you to be aware of the possible danger." Her sharp eyes narrowed on him. "Do you intend on keeping it from her?"

Jasper hesitated. His protective instincts roared for him to do exactly that, but his brain insisted that she would not take kindly to his interference *or* hiding it from her. He wanted to safeguard her, but there was also a healthy respect for the fact that she was a grown adult with a perfectly functioning brain of her own.

Minthe cleared her throat at his protracted silence, a look of censure flashing across her face. "Please tell me I wasn't wrong in coming to you, my lord. Lady Briar should know. I only came here first because I was not certain that she would be here today, and this seemed urgent."

"No, you're right," he said quickly to dispel her worry. "Of course, I agree that she should know. While I wish to keep her from harm, she can make her own choices, regardless of whether I like them or not."

Minthe's exhale was loud. "That's what I thought. Thank you for not disappointing me by being yet another man who thinks he knows what is best, especially for a woman."

"Never," he said, scrubbing a hand over his jaw. He offered up a small smile. "Besides, she'd skewer me, wouldn't she?"

"Without any doubt."

As if their discussion had summoned her, Briar burst through the door of his office, a tempest in brilliant buttercup-yellow, and Jasper caught his breath. Even in the wake of such a disquieting message, she was like a beam of sunlight in the darkness, and everything inside of him brightened as though *he'd* been stuck in the dark for an eternity, starved from the sight of her.

No, no, no.

Jasper clenched his jaw. Now was clearly not the time to be quixotic, but he also did not want to pick apart the sense of *ease* unraveling in his chest. Safe, he always needed her to be safe. Regrettably and to his everlasting frustration, she was someone who usually cared more about *others'* safety than her own. That lack of self-preservation was the only reason that he'd hesitated with Minthe before.

"I beg your pardon," Briar said, that emerald gaze sliding uncertainly between them. "Am I interrupting something?"

"No, my lady, I was just leaving."

Shooting him a meaningful look, Minthe took her leave with a passing squeeze of Briar's arm. It was incongruous to think that a high-born peeress would be bosom friends with a former courtesan, considering most of the *ton's* views on women of Minthe's station and profession, but Briar had never looked down on any of them. She let their character speak for them instead of their circumstances.

Jasper had asked her why once, and she had glared at him as though he were in the wrong for even asking, stating that anyone could fall prey to misfortune, and if a person had to survive by any means necessary, then who were they to judge them? Nobility of birth did not guarantee nobility of spirit, she'd stated, and her impassioned conviction had always stuck with him. It was one of the many things he admired about Briar: her ability to see past a person's exterior.

It was also one of the things that could lead her into trouble.

Not *everyone* was as kind or had altruistic motives.

Case in point—the person who clearly had ill intentions by sending her the message still crumpled in his fist. Before he could stupidly change his mind, he smoothed the parchment out and handed it to her.

"What is this?" she asked, taking it.

"Minthe said it came for you earlier. It wasn't in an envelope. She brought it to me because she wasn't sure that you would be here today."

Briar scanned the two lines with a tiny frown appearing between her brows. "This was delivered here for *me*?"

Jasper nodded. "Can you think of who it might be from? Or why anyone would send a message like that?"

"No, but it certainly seems untoward, if slightly disturbing," Briar said, pacing the carpet and peering at him. "No one I know calls me *little dove*. How peculiar. Are you certain this was meant for me and not someone else?

He shook his head. "Minthe confirmed the messenger said your name."

"Could he have been mistaken?" she pressed.

"He could have, I suppose, but we don't have any other Lady Briars who come and go as they please from this establishment."

"So, it would be smart to assume that someone has been watching me." She chewed her lip and dropped the piece of parchment on the desk. "And they want me to know that they have been."

Jaw clenched, he nodded. "I would presume so, yes."

To his utter horror, her lower lip started to wobble. *Briar*...who never displayed any kind of weakness whatsoever. He blinked, but her expression of anguish didn't disappear, the mask of cheer she'd worn vanishing completely. Something was *wrong*, and he'd been so taken in by her presence that he hadn't noticed the faint smudges beneath her eyes or their unusually dimmed depths.

"This is bad, Jasper. I can feel it."

He jolted as the tenor of his given name crossed her lips. She only ever called him that here, where they dispensed with formality. But it was the break in her voice that gave him pause coupled with the sudden tightness of her shoulders. He'd known her long enough to realize that she was teetering on the edge of control, hanging on by a thread. This wasn't like her. She was always full of positive banter with a lively personality and rarely let anyone see her crumble. Not even Vesper and her friends.

Not like this.

He rose and walked over to her, gathering her taut frame into his arms. She stiffened further, hiding her face against his shirtfront.

"W...what are you doing?" she mumbled, though she made no attempt to pull away.

He tightened his arms. "Hugging you."

Briar didn't say a word, but he could feel her shallow tremors and the ragged dissonance of her breaths. He dipped his chin to rest on the soft spirals over her crown, inhaling her alluring jasmine scent just as a ragged half sob ripped from her.

"Tell me what's really wrong," he said.

He didn't think she was going to answer, but then her entire body seemed to slump. "Did you see the newssheets?" she whispered. "The viscount's engagement to Lady Penelope?" Glossy green eyes lifted to his, and he resisted the urge to stroke her cheek. "I'm so sorry," she added. "I know you had been courting her and intended to wed. You must be disappointed."

"I don't care about me. I care about you." Jasper tightened his arms and pressed his mouth in a ghost of a kiss to the soft skin of her forehead. "I assume from your reaction that he cried off. He's an idiot. What happened?"

"He caught me distributing pamphlets for the Society for Women's Suffrage the other morning, and well, he's against all of that," Briar said, shoulders heaving. "He thinks it's blasphemous. That men and women were created to be in our separate positions. Man in a position of dominance, and woman in one of subservience."

Jasper wanted to roll his eyes. No surprise there. The viscount was a sanctimonious git whose dogmatic opinions were stuck in the Middle Ages. But like many other men, he didn't see women as people; he saw them as property. How someone as intelligent as Briar hadn't foreseen this was a shock to him, but that was neither here nor there. She needed comfort, not condemnation. "I'm sorry," he said.

"And he...saw us dancing at the ball," she said softly. She lifted tremulous, tear-filled eyes to his, and he nudged a curl out of her brow. "He was furious."

"Was he? From a dance?"

"Yes." Her gaze dropped to his mouth for an interminable moment, and her eyelashes fluttered before she suddenly went rigid as though belatedly realizing what she was doing. "I'm sorry, I'm not usually like this."

"Stay, Briar," he whispered, keeping his hold tight when she made to pull away. Whether or not she would admit it, she needed comfort. Both from what had happened with that varlet and the humiliation of such a public announce-ment that had been meant to hurt. Briar was right—she wasn't usually like this, but even the thickest of walls could be fractured with the right force.

"I'm fine," she said. "Let me go, Lushing."

"No."

"You're being bloody annoying."

"You love me when I'm annoying," he said into the soft mass of her hair, the band of his arms unrelenting.

She glared up at him, but there was little heat in it, and if he wasn't mistaken, the tension seemed to seep further from her body as her muscles relaxed infinitesimally into his. After another beat, her eyes fluttered closed and she turned her cheek into his chest with a near inaudible sigh. Jasper suppressed his satisfaction. She didn't often let him hold her or perform any displays of outward affection, so he would take the wins where he could get them.

He'd hold her forever if he had to.

Minutes or an eternity later, she stirred, and this time Jasper released her.

"Thank you," she whispered stiffly. "I apologize. I did not expect to be so overcome."

"No need. It was no hardship on my part," he said with a smile, watching as she dabbed at her face and smoothed her hair back into place. "About the engagement..."

In an instant, the ease fled from her body as her spine snapped straight, ready for battle. A sparking, furious green gaze slammed into his, and Jasper lifted his hands in instant surrender.

"Before you skewer me, Sweetbriar, I have a proposition that might get us both what we want."

"A pretense?" Briar frowned, staring at him in shock. "Of a fake courtship?"

"Yes," the earl said bluntly. "Do you want Sackley back?"

Briar blinked out of the semi-stupor, her brain wavering with indecision before she sighed with a nod. "Well, there's the matter of the dowry of the Bath estate and the eventual combination of the land."

She knew it was an evasive answer, and Lushing, for all

his devil-may-care ways, was not a stupid man. It was one thing that others underestimated about him. They saw a lighthearted rogue who had a laissez-faire attitude about life and deemed him no one to take seriously. But Lushing had a brain that rivaled the genius of renowned scholars. His memory was unmatched. He retained everything...*every* little detail, and while such a talent could be infuriating at times, especially when he reminded her of things she'd said years ago, Briar esteemed him for it.

"Then what do you have to lose?" he asked.

What *did* she have to lose?

Her brows converged. She was still trying to collect herself after being held by the warmest, most muscled pair of arms she'd ever felt and how unfairly *divine* it had been to be surrounded by all that steady, fortifying strength. The rich woodsy scent of him still lingered in her nose. His embrace had felt like serenity...like nothing could ever harm her while she was there. She'd shamelessly indulged in it, though every decadent second had made her question her own lack of good sense.

He was not *hers*.

Though to his earlier point, neither of them was anyone's. They'd both been jilted for other people. Truth be told, she hadn't properly processed what had happened or how quickly Preston had moved on to greener and clearly much less *vulgar* pastures. Briar swallowed her bitterness. Lady Penelope would never last on the filthy streets of Seven Dials, much less set a foot beyond the pristine cobblestones of Mayfair to help someone in need. And yet, she was the preference...the very soul of propriety and decorum. The bloody diamond of the season.

It was the principle of it, really. The public message the viscount's rejection sent—that something was *wrong* with Briar.

Dear God, her parents, who'd been so pleased about the engagement, must be horrified. Briar couldn't begin to imagine the shame and embarrassment her poor mother would feel at the news and the gossip that would undoubtedly be spreading faster than wildfire. The fact that her own daughter wasn't enough...

No. Those pejorative feelings weren't useful. She needed to think. Briar inhaled a deep, bracing breath, her resentment lessening as she considered Lushing's proposition. She could salvage this. She *would*—all her plans depended on it.

She'd make Preston *see* that she was the better choice. The only choice.

Somehow.

Admittedly, it was hard to be optimistic when both men, the earl opposite her *and* her former fiancé, coveted the same woman. Lushing had been courting her, and Preston had proposed to her.

But the outrageous idea had merit.

Lushing was heir to a duke, which meant he was desirable and eligible. He outranked Preston, and that would needle the viscount to no end, if played correctly. He might be pious, but he was also prideful. It was obvious from all the poisonous jabs he made at the *ton*...her friends and the Earl of Lushing, in particular. And men, even sanctimonious ones, thrived on competition.

Briar gnawed her lip. This...might just work.

As if he could sense her near capitulation to the outlandish but brilliant idea, the earl strode to where she stood near the stuffed bookcase on the other side of his office. "It's a win-win for both of us," he said. "You get your fiancé and childhood home back, and I get the betrothal I worked so hard for all these weeks. We can help each other, Briar."

Ignoring the extraordinarily pleasurable pulse she felt at the sound of her given name on his lips, she released a slow breath. Did he truly want Penelope back so badly? "Do you fancy Lady Penelope?" she blurted. "I mean, she doesn't seem like...your usual"—she coughed delicately— "preference."

The smirk that curled his lips was criminal, making heat dissipate into unmentionable parts of her. "My *preference*?" he repeated in a voice like velvet. "Keeping tabs on me, Prickles?"

Goodness, why did her entire body feel like it was melting?

She jutted her chin. "How are you this insufferable? No, I do not, but you do seem to prefer ladies of the demimonde. Your last paramour was an opera singer, if I recall." Not that she was cataloguing his love interests. Briar felt her face warm with embarrassment, a fact she was sure he didn't miss. "Flamboyant and bold. Experienced. Not at all prim and proper, or anyone your father would approve of as a society wife."

"Perhaps that's the appeal then," he replied smoothly. "I required a lady whom the duke would favor without much fuss, and I suppose Lady Penelope fits the bill nicely. She's the perfect lady in the *ton's* eyes. She is the season's diamond, after all."

Briar nodded, a lump of something bitter growing in her

throat. Nothing like *her*, clearly. Preston's harsh words came back to haunt her, and she viciously buried those feelings of insufficiency. At least Briar had a brain. She knew she was being petty, but she didn't care. Luckily, a person's thoughts were private. She was a lady, and despite her unconventional extracurricular activities, she was of the same rank as Lady Penelope. They were *both* daughters of peers.

"Very well," she said. "What do you propose? We pretend to be affianced?"

The earl tapped his chin. "Courting should suffice for now. An engagement means involving your parents out of respect. I will take every opportunity to flaunt the point that a discerning lady of your elevated station is positively unaffected by the shocking and gauche betrothal news in the viscount's face, and that I was quick to snatch up the true prize he so stupidly let go of. Let's make him think *he* has lost something of immeasurable value."

"Which he has, *obviously*," she said with burgeoning bravado.

Eyes sparkling, he sent her a sidelong glance. "That's the spirit."

Briar reached for resolve. "In turn, I shall vociferously celebrate the fact that I am *relieved* to be courted by a handsome, debonair earl versus a mere viscount. The *ton* will relish the shallowness of such a sentiment."

"A very rich earl who is the heir to a solvent, thriving dukedom," Lushing added and then grinned, those deep blue eyes glinting with mischief as he threw a theatrical hand to his heart. "Handsome *and* debonair? Why, Sweetbriar, you might be obsessed with me..."

And there he was, Narcissus in the flesh.

Briar huffed and rolled her eyes. "It is a ruse, Lushing. By definition, a *lie*. I shall have to work extra hard to get past your dreadful personality and your bloated ego. Obsession is the furthest thing from the truth."

Flexing his chest—his very hard, muscular chest that she could still feel the warmth of against her cheek—the scoundrel winked. "Keep telling yourself that."

"When do we start this farce?"

He looked entirely too pleased. "Tomorrow night. The opera. Let's give the *ton* a spectacle they've never seen."

She had to admit, his zeal was contagious. If they could pull this off, it would be the accomplishment of the season. "Why? Who are we making jealous?"

"Everyone, Sweetbriar. Everyone."

CHAPTER FIVE

"Fuck me."

They were the only words that could escape Jasper's lips as he stood at the top of the grand staircase of the Royal Opera House in conversation with the Marquess and Marchioness of Marsden while waiting for his new accomplice to arrive. And arrive she had in an entrance that would not soon be forgotten. The wind blew in around her, lifting the voluptuous waterfall of the long bronze spirals spilling over her exposed golden-brown shoulders like aged cognac.

His mouth dried, lungs squeezing as the organ in his chest started a thunderous throb.

Chatter in the foyer sputtered out.

Briar Fairview was indisputably a beautiful woman, but *this* wasn't just a beautiful woman. This was a fucking queen in crimson, and like everyone else, all he could do was gasp and stare. He drank her in like a man stuck in the desert dying of thirst. She hadn't come to make anyone jealous; she'd come here to make them kneel.

In a sea of pastels and whites, the red was an audacious,

undeniably powerful choice, one designed to command every eye in the room. The square bodice clung to her décolletage, the cascade of a hundred silk-petaled, blood-red moiré roses tumbling over the layers that fell from her cinched waist. But the gown, as stunning as it was in scarlet silk faille that ran like liquid flame over those voluptuous curves, paled in comparison to the woman who wore it. It was simply an accessory like the rubies glittering at her ears and throat.

He could feel the caress of that bright emerald gaze when it finally found him, and their eyes crashed and held. Blood rushed between his ears as something decidedly elemental sizzled in the air like a kiss of lightning. He felt electrified. Thunderstruck.

It was *her*...she was the storm.

Time stopped, his breath hissing past his teeth in an endless exhale when she smiled with the confidence of a goddess who knew the world was hers for the taking. Jasper wanted to drop to his knees like a willing supplicant...and beg for her favor. Beg for *anything*.

"Goodness, is that Briar?" Lady Marsden said, breaking the strange spell that had come over him. "She's a vision!"

Without answering, Jasper bolted down the stairs two at a time like an unrefined lout, forcing a smirk to his lips instead of the awe that kept them slack when he stood in front of her. "I said make them jealous, Prickles, not slay everyone in the immediate vicinity."

Pleasure sparked in her eyes before she canted her head. "Good evening, my lord," she said, those full lips quirking upward and conspiring to make him brainless. *Again*. "I gather there's a compliment buried in there somewhere."

"You're fucking stunning and you know it," he said, and her green eyes glowed. Her laugh was a husky sound that should never be allowed outside of a bedchamber. Jasper fought the urge to adjust his already crowded trousers.

"Thank you, my lord. You clean up well yourself."

Jasper knew he cut a decent figure in his raven-black formalwear that was tailored to his frame, but he basked in the appreciative look in her gaze as it swung languidly from his hat to the tips of his gleaming shoes. He offered her his arm. "Shall we?"

He felt the avid interest of every single stare in the room from men and women alike—covetous, jealous, admiring, curious—as they ascended the staircase to where he'd left their friends so abruptly.

"Apologies for being an utter troglodyte," he said, patting the gloved forearm that curled around his. "I needed to stake my claim before anyone else did."

His companion blushed, the tinge of pink a direct contrast to the boldness of the gown she wore. Entranced, Jasper watched that mesmerizing flush distill over her collarbones until a discreet cough interrupted him.

"Lady Briar," the marquess greeted. "Always a pleasure to see you."

"And you, my lord," she replied before turning to her friend. "You look lovely, Laila."

"As do you," the marchioness said as they embraced. "I didn't know you were coming tonight. Lushing intimated that he had invited someone to accompany him, but I did not expect you. We could have offered you a ride in our coach." She glanced at Jasper. "Speaking of that, why didn't she come with you?"

Jasper arched a brow, lips curling upward. "Then my fiancée's entrance would not have been so spectacular, would it?" The declaration had left his lips before he could stop it. Ignoring the sharp inhales of both women as well as his own fucking conscience, he continued, "As though a certain gauche announcement in the newssheets was of no consequence whatsoever."

"I gather congratulations are in order then," Marsden said slowly, oblivious to his wife's concern. Briar stared at him in stupefaction but didn't contradict him.

"Thank you," Jasper said, casting a discreet glance to where people were looking at them and whispering. "Everyone should know that the indomitable Lady Briar Fairview wasted no time on a dunghill like Viscount Sackley and is now betrothed to *me*, the most eligible bachelor in London."

Briar shot him a quelling look when several more spectators around them swiveled in their direction. He *was* laying it on rather thickly. But wasn't that the whole point of the charade? In for a penny, in for a pound then. Jasper lifted her hand to his mouth and bussed his lips over her knuckles before tucking her possessively into his side.

Dead silence ensued.

"Fiancée," Laila repeated, her gaze flying to her friend. To Briar's credit, she quickly nodded, though Jasper knew she was mystified by his turnabout. He'd said no to an engagement as part of the ruse, not thinking it necessary, but now, the distinction seemed vital.

Something in him calmed when she gave an easy shrug. "It's not announced," she explained to the marchioness. "We wanted the news to be between us for a bit."

Lady Marsden's eyes swung between them, her eyebrows climbing into her hairline. "Wait, you're serious—?"

"It's new," Briar said. "Actually, it was something Vesper said at the ball that we all attended. After the engagement announcement came out with the viscount and Lady Penelope, naturally, I was devastated, but I suppose it was a blessing in disguise because Lord Lushing and I realized that we might be better suited." She waved a casual hand, sending him a shy smile that was so unlike her that *he* almost frowned. "You know how capricious these things can be."

"Capricious," her friend echoed, elegant brows crashing.

Briar slid her arm into the crook of his, her scent curling into his nostrils as she squeezed lightly. "Yes, exactly. The heart wants what the heart wants."

"But you don't *like* him," she whispered to Briar. "In fact, your *heart* categorically abhors him. You've declared it often enough, *especially* when Vesper suggests that there's anything between the two of you." Her voice lowered. "And now you're *engaged*?"

Briar gave a rueful but authentic smile. "We don't call her Cupidella for nothing. She's brilliant at matchmaking. Perhaps un grand amour, as Nève calls it, was in front of us all along and we were both too pigheaded to see it."

"Un grand amour?" Lady Marsden repeated as though it were a curse.

"Be happy for me, Laila," Briar said with a gentle laugh.

The marchioness immediately looked contrite. "I *am*."

Briar was so convincing that Jasper wanted to applaud her performance. She was just the right amount of sweet bashfulness with a healthy dash of the sass she was known for. But if Lady Marsden could manage to look any more incredulous, her jaw might unhinge and fall to the floor. Surely an engagement between the two of them wasn't *so* preposterous, but the marquess's expression was just as confounded as his wife's. Fortunately, men didn't opine on these things. Wooing a lady was usually a matter of business.

Well, except for Marsden, whose wife had shoved him into the Serpentine. And Montcroix, who had paid his ballerina to be his fake fiancée but discovered she was the love of his life. Also, Greydon, who had convinced Vesper to matchmake his ward, only to realize his own infatuation. Not to mention Vale, who had made an absurd wager to trick Effie into going to London and ended up falling tail-over-top for her.

Jasper sighed. Not always a matter of business, then.

Well, bully for them. He and Briar would be the exception. No buffoonery. No falling in lakes, wagers, or paid arrangements, just an agreement between friends. Once their goal was accomplished, they would go their separate ways and back to their temperamental partnership.

As she savored the sound of the beautiful soprano soaring to the rafters, Briar smoothed the silky fabric of her dress. Her racing heart hadn't settled one bit. Trust Lushing to take things a step—*several steps*—too far. Now, they were affianced. She should be irate at the sudden change in plans, but she didn't feel too upset about it. In fact, she didn't want to dwell on the curious swell of pleasure in her chest.

The dratted engagement wasn't real.

He'd obviously wanted to sell the performance for a good reason. Had the gown been too much? Briar frowned. She could still feel the attention from other onlookers staring into the Earl of Lushing's private box from behind their fans and fingers. She'd wanted to make a statement that she was undaunted by the actions of her former fiancé, and she had.

Conclusively.

It wasn't *just* the dress, however, that was making her breathless. It was the lethally charismatic earl who sat to her right, his presence a ridiculous contradiction of being both soothing and unsettling. Her senses veered between comfort and alarm—comfort that he was a steady, dependable force in this whole farce and alarm that she was so grievously, stupidly attracted to him.

Briar couldn't remember being so aware of every nerve in her body, so much so that the occasional shiver quaked through her frame. She was certain he could feel it, as he'd inquired several times if she was cold, especially when the truth was, she was immolating from the inside.

Had she ever truly realized how handsome the earl was? How tall and fit and elegant? How that lean boxer's body— she'd seen him fight in the ring at Lethe with the enormous Duke of Vale *and* hold his own—flexed beneath the bespoke suit he wore. She was accustomed to seeing him at Lethe and on the seedy streets of London.

A business owner and reluctant protector, not this dashing suitor.

The man was a chameleon. His jokes and affability tended to disarm...and people, especially criminals, didn't realize they were in the sights of a predator until it was much too late. He wore the guise of an unassuming, amiable peer, but the bruised, scarred knuckles beneath the expensive leather gloves said he was anything but indolent. He was blade wrapped in velvet, beautiful to look at but just as deadly, and the combination was deeply seductive.

And this was all fake, she reminded herself.

And yet...

Had she ever noticed how sharp his jawline was? Or admired the rich auburn streaks in his hair that glinted garnet in the gaslights? Or how the full curve of that sensual bottom lip disappeared and reappeared glistening from between his teeth? How she wanted to taste it so badly that her mouth watered.

Sure, she had imagined him as a faceless fantasy many a time, but it was as though she'd never *seen* him before. Never *felt* him so acutely before. Not like this.

Her nipples were beaded in her bodice, her inner thighs so damp with arousal that she kept her legs pinned tightly together. She wished she had a notebook so she could write down her feelings. As an author, nothing went to waste...and this was all inspiration for Lady Ivy.

In truth, Briar had been channeling Lady Ivy when she'd chosen the dress. The heiress-turned-courtesan was beautiful and had confidence in spades. The entire world was her playground, its occupants hers to command and there for her pleasure. Briar had never done that before: assumed the identity of her fictional creation, but it was unexpectedly, deliciously liberating.

So much so that she wanted things she had no business craving...

Briar lifted her fan and waved it furiously, hoping to dissipate some of the heat. She could feel the perspiration sliding between her breasts, their sensitivity almost unbearable. Squirming slightly in her chair, she sensed the earl's attention upon her once more.

"Are you well?" his deep baritone whispered into her right ear.

God, the heat of his breath felt like a caress against her lobe that arrowed right to her peaked nipples and sank lower to where she *ached*.

"Yes," she breathed out. "It's a bit warm."

"Intermission will be soon," he said and then pressed his head even closer, his lips nearly grazing her excruciatingly sensitive skin. Briar suppressed another shiver. "Sackley and Penelope are here," Lushing murmured. "In the box directly across to the right. Don't look now. He hasn't taken his eyes off you since our arrival."

Sucking in a sharp breath, Briar lifted her fan and discreetly glanced over the embroidered edge of lace. Sure enough, Preston's gaze was fastened to their box instead of the stage. It gave Briar great satisfaction to know that Penelope also kept darting fraught glances full of uncertainty to the earl beside her.

Was she also regretting her decision? What had Preston told her about the earl to get her to capitulate so quickly and accept his suit? It had to have been something terrible. The Earl of Lushing's reputation wasn't pristine or a secret. Everyone knew about Lethe, and Jasper had always been an unrepentant rake who flouted the rules of high society to do as he pleased.

Men could be worse gossips than women.

From the thin line of his lips, the viscount was fuming. Though why he was angry was a mystery. *He* had broken it off with her for being too vulgar, for handing out a few pamphlets, and having the audacity to dance with a friend. Had he expected her to come crawling back to him...to beg for his forgiveness and plead for him to take her back? Perhaps he had. Briar had quietly taken his sly pinches, after all, as well as his spiteful jibes. But she had been so focused on securing her future that none of that had mattered.

She blinked. If Lushing hadn't suggested this asinine plan, maybe she would have swallowed her dignity and done exactly that. *Begged* him to take her back. Her stomach twisted. Goodness, was she truly that eager to marry such a craven man, even if it guaranteed her independence? The answer had always been yes. Her work with the women and her writing mattered more than a pinch or two or a pathetic insult. Preston had been nothing but a tool.

A name to give her existence as a woman basic legitimacy.

Because they were invisible without a fucking husband.

Heat crept up her neck again, but this time it was for a different reason. She was furious and frustrated that she had to even engineer something like this just to have the life she wanted. Women should be able to choose their futures for themselves, not depend on a husband who may or may not be open-minded. They were real persons with their own hopes and dreams. Why *should* they need a man to exist fully? It was nonsensical.

She rose, her corset growing unbearably tight. "Excuse me."

"Lady Briar?" Lushing asked with concern, also standing.

"I'm fine, but I need a moment," she said, meeting Laila's

gaze and giving an infinitesimal jerk of her chin. "I'll just be a minute. Laila will be with me, don't worry."

Gulping huge breaths into her lungs, she practically ran from the box to the nearest retiring room. Thankfully, the space was nearby and empty. Briar splashed water on her face just as Laila entered behind her.

"Briar, what's wrong?" her friend asked, eyes dark with worry.

"Nothing. I couldn't breathe for a moment, and my vision started swimming. I was afraid I was going to swoon. I *never* faint." She hunched over the basin and clasped a hand over her chest, pressing hard into her breastbone as if the pressure could alleviate the constriction of her lungs.

Laila rubbed her back before drawing her to sit on a small settee. "Is it because of the engagement with the earl? Tell me the truth. Is it real?"

The loaded questions made her breaths even shallower, but Briar knew she had to sell the performance, or all of this would be for naught. The retiring room might be empty of guests, but there were still attendants close by as well as footmen in the corridors outside. In the *ton*, there were ears and eyes everywhere, even when one did not see them.

"It is," she said and carefully considered her words. "I know it might seem as though I haven't thought things through, considering what you already know of my feelings for him, but Lushing is a good man underneath all the vanity and posturing. I'm safe."

Laila nodded, though her face still looked uncertain. "We both know that Vesper would commit fratricide without hesitation, if he ever put one toe out of line or does anything to harm a hair on your head." She sucked in a breath. "But that doesn't mean that you're right for each other. This is impulsive, even for you. And you've just been through a shock—anyone would be upset over Viscount Sackley's heartless actions. Perhaps you should take some time before rushing into another courtship." She worried her lip. "If this is some creative way to save face with the *ton*, then that's different."

She was so close to the truth that Briar nearly gave it all away—her nostrils were stinging with the urge to burst into tears—but by some miracle, she kept her expression blank. She had to give her friend *something*. After so many years of friendship, Laila knew her much too well to simply believe she'd had such a change of heart with Lushing, of all people. "You're right. I was hurt, but Sackley was always a means to an end. The earl and I have discovered a mutual esteem. He needs a wife, and I need a husband. And he's not so terrible, once you get to know him."

And he makes my heart race in ways I cannot explain...

She squashed that down immediately. Her feelings of attraction were unrequited. The earl wanted Penelope.

Laila sniffed. "You *do* know him, Briar. He's Lushing. A rogue. A charming, rakish scoundrel with nothing but idleness on his mind. I adore him and he's diverting company, but by God, he's...*Lushing*."

"You say his name like a reductive adjective," Briar said, lips twitching with humor.

"Isn't it?"

She wasn't wrong. "He's tolerable then."

Laila barked a laugh. "In the words of Austen, *barely*. That's the bar of what we're aiming for these days?"

Briar laughed, the knot in her chest finally loosening.

"We can't all find a gentleman to shove into the Serpentine to make them fall hopelessly in love with us."

"That was an *accident*."

"Clearly, a happy accident," Briar said. "Perhaps love will find us the way it did you and Marsden. All I must do is find a lake to drown Lushing in. With a custom pair of cement boots." Laila's eyes went wide, and Briar snorted, feeling lighter for the first time since seeing Preston's awful announcement. "I'm only jesting. Partly. If he vexes me too much and I suddenly purchase a boat, you may intervene."

"You are terrible," Laila said, hand over her mouth to stifle her giggles.

"See? I'm barely tolerable myself. The earl and I are meant to be." Briar embraced the marchioness, holding her tightly. "I promise all will be well, Laila. You have nothing to worry about, but I love you for looking out for me."

"I always will," she said and squeezed even harder before pulling away with a teary smile. "But for a second, can we talk about this *gown*? You are a siren. Whoever made this fascinating concoction must be a dressmaking genius."

Briar winked. "Well, yes, considering said genius is only the most iconic designer and modiste of all time. You made this years ago, if you recall, for one of Vesper's themed masquerades, and I never ended up wearing it because I fell ill," she said, glancing down at her plentiful décolletage spilling over the top. "Though it's now a bit tight."

Laila shot her a wicked grin. "It's perfect. The girls would perish if they saw you right now, though I'm sure there will be a detailed likeness in the newspaper tomorrow." She stroked the hand-stitched roses with fondness. "I remember now. These took me forever; silk can be so uncooperative, but the effect was worth every pricked finger. If you planned to make a grand statement about what you thought of the announcement, it was loud and clear. The viscount couldn't take his eyes off you."

"I saw," Briar said. "But this wasn't for him. It was for me. I wanted to feel powerful and untouchable, and this gown accomplished that, so thank you."

"You're welcome. Now if you've sufficiently recovered enough to breathe, let's get back before the marquess sends out a search party. I swear the man cannot bear to be away from me for more than a handful of minutes."

Briar felt a pulse of envy, but she waggled her eyebrows playfully as they rose and smoothed their dresses. "Tell me your secrets, oh great one. Lady Ivy needs all the motivation she can get."

Laila's face went the color of Briar's dress. "Suffice it to say that *Lady Ivy* is the reason he's so happy of late."

They were both so wrapped up in their chortles that they didn't hear the knock or the door opening until a throat cleared. Briar's eyes clashed with a pair of sparkling blues that stole her breath, and she couldn't quite contain the indecent rush of pleasure that it was him and not Marsden. Laila widened her eyes comically and then skirted around the earl to make her escape.

"I became concerned when you did not return," he said, entering and closing the door behind him.

"This is a retiring room for *ladies*, my lord," she said, his huge form dominating the space, that cedar-and-spice scent besetting her nostrils as he closed the distance between them. God, would it be rude to inhale deeply for a handful of minutes? It was simply not fair for a man to smell so good.

"I am aware." His fingers lifted to brush a loose spiral of hair from her cheek. "Is all well?"

"It is now," she said. "But perhaps we shouldn't court scandal so blatantly just yet by being caught in here together alone. A swift march to the altar defeats the purpose, does it not?"

"Would that be so bad?" he murmured.

She gaped. Was he jesting? Pretending they were engaged was all well and good, but tying herself to him for better or for worse—likely for *worse*—would be an irrevocable mistake. Briar ignored the burst of heat in her core when wicked visions of a wedding night filled with writhing bodies and entangled limbs followed.

Her eyelids fluttered as she ducked her head to hide her indecent thoughts. "I suspect neither of us would survive the conflagration. We would burn each other to ash."

"Ah, but what a glorious way to go." He smirked as if her private musings were entirely transparent and opened the door. "But you're right, it would defeat the purpose."

Confused by the faint sound of regret in his tone, she frowned up at him as he led her back to their box. "Don't you want Lady Penelope back?"

"Not particularly," he said, and her eyes flew wide. "She humiliated me."

"So, you *don't* want her?" she asked carefully.

"I want her to crawl and then I'll decide."

Taken aback, Briar stared at him, a shiver running through her at the utter dearth of emotion in his tone. Lushing might be fun and games on the surface, but he had a thread of darkness in him that ran deep. It was a streak of ruthlessness that he didn't display often, but one she'd seen from time to time at Lethe when members violated his rules or put their hands on his employees, and that kind of protective dominance had always made her stupidly weak.

The sudden image of *her* on her knees at a gravelly command nearly had her falling flat on her face.

"Bloody hell, sorry. There was a bump in the carpet."

"Careful, love," Lushing said, with a serene smile and a gentle clasp on her arm that belied his earlier vicious words. "So, who's Lady Ivy?"

CHAPTER SIX

The answer to Jasper's question from the other night at the opera lay in his hands: a slim novel entitled *Lady Ivy Thorn, Or A Study in Secrets.* He sucked in a breath as he traced the simple design and plain lettering on the red leather-bound cover with one finger. It seemed ordinary enough. These sensation novels were taking London by storm—mysteries, crime fiction, and gothic romances—all with one thing in common...shocking subject matter like adultery, revenge, robbery, murder, romance, and seduction.

There was no author's name, but he knew this was Briar with every fiber of his being. Even the name of the titular character was close to one of his own playful nicknames. His mouth quirked. It had taken many hours of perusing literary magazines, and visiting bookstores and newsstands before he'd finally, inadvertently overheard a gaggle of older women at a tea shop discussing the contents of a new Lady Ivy book in fervent whispers.

It was only with infinite patience that he'd waited until they had finished before innocently bumping into the woman with the volume in hand and gallantly apologizing for his clumsiness...but not before getting a thorough look at the cover and title.

"You dropped this, Miss," he'd said with his characteristic charm, halting himself at the last minute from stooping to petty thievery. It was one thing to shamelessly eavesdrop and another to steal someone's personal property. "Lord Lushing, at your service," he'd said with a smart bow as he handed her the book. "I do love a good mystery. A Study in Secrets sounds rather exciting. Would I enjoy this one?"

She had stared at him with huge eyes, her face going the color of a beet. "Y...yes, my lord. Though *no*, categorically not...it's for l...ladies. I doubt you would...er...goodbye."

Book snatched and tucked into a pocket, she'd rushed off rather quickly.

And now, after sending his factotum on a wild goose chase that ended on Holywell Street where salacious bookshops sold racy literature to locate his own copy. Shockingly, Lady Ivy had sold out the printing of five hundred copies in days, but a few creative bribes later, Jasper was finally holding the slender red volume in his hands. This genre of work, novel-with-a-secret, was aptly called sensation fiction, and they were the rage.

He closed the door to his office and made himself comfortable in his chair.

"What are you hiding, Sweetbriar?" he murmured, and turned to the first page. He started reading. The story was whimsical and charming, the tale of an affluent but bored French heiress who had become a widow after a very short marriage. Though she was wealthy and a woman of independent means, she decided to become a governess.

Interesting choice, though Jasper couldn't quite understand why a rich widow would choose such a profession. He continued reading and found himself swiftly turning the pages. Despite being a young, widowed aristocrat, the heroine was relatable across class and station, considering her own humble origins as a shopkeeper's daughter. Perhaps that was why she chose to become a governess, though that plot point still didn't make sense to him as there were no children. Perhaps they would come later in the story.

Considering Briar's vast intelligence coupled with her flair for dramatics, she was a lyrical and descriptive writer—he could almost hear her voice reciting the words. The narrative was so much like Briar that he found himself smiling as he read, her social commentary about the glittering world she lived in clever and satirical. She communicated in a way that felt accessible, weaving a story that any woman could relate to—one of hopes and dreams, and being true to herself, in a world that offered their sex little autonomy. Even *he* felt connected to the heroine. Self-discovery was universal, after all.

In the second chapter, Lady Ivy visited a special chamber in her grand house. A room that catered to the exploration of...voluptuous fantasies. Jasper blinked, rereading the words.

Surely, Briar didn't mean...

But on the next page, when Lady Ivy boldly removed her robe upon entering the chamber that was wallpapered in hues of black, cream, and red, Jasper's neck went hot. She was described as wearing soft kidskin boots that climbed from her soles to her thighs, lace coverings resembling ivy leaves over her hips and chest, and a demi-mask. In one hand, she held a riding crop that she tapped against the top of her boot. Her smile was one of unguarded desire as she surveyed the domain, including the handsome copper-haired lover who waited bonded and gagged, saying, "Your governess demands obedience."

Tugging at his collar, Jasper blinked and blinked again. So, when she wrote governess, Briar had meant *that* kind of governess...like the ones specializing in flagellation in Marylebone who were experts in inflicting pain with pleasure. Every drop of blood in his body descended immediately to his cock. Dear *God*. He'd expected some broad strokes of amorousness, perhaps some heaving bosoms and a display of an ankle or two, but never this. Loosening his cravat and adjusting himself, he continued reading.

Aside from the explicit nature of Lady Ivy's adventures, it *was* exceptionally written...the descriptive details were truly a study in secrets and sensuality. The brisk honesty of the prose, juxtaposed with the air of innocence of the main character, was an intriguing combination. The dialogue was witty and audacious, just like the author, and Jasper found himself laughing out loud in parts, his heart pounding in others. The undercurrent of arousal that ran through the story felt like an entirely separate character—an omniscient one—as if desire were a companion on a journey.

Jasper could not help himself; he was hooked. He kept reading. An hour flew by, and then another. By the time he finished consuming the entire story of Lady Ivy's adventures, he was sweating, his body was teetering on the knife-edge of arousal, and he had a raging cockstand that showed zero signs of dissipating. In fact, he was harder than he'd ever been in his life.

He'd had to stop and go back to several sections, all the while unable to comprehend in the most primal, animalistic part of his brain that *Briar*—feisty, fierce, *inexperienced* Briar Fairview—was the author of something so sensually lush and extraordinarily vivid.

It didn't seem possible, given her innocence, and yet, he knew it was her.

She isn't that innocent...

Not only did Lady Ivy dispense and desire praise, degradation, and punishment from her lover, all depicted with very explicit consent and care, but she relished every second of it, open to truly embracing each part of the hedonistic experience. It was evident that the gentle, rhapsodic prose underscoring such sensational material was written for women in mind, with the subtle encouragement for them to ask for what they wanted with their partners...and to amplify that they, too, were deserving of pleasure.

That pleasure was a gift.

Briar was, without a doubt, a talented storyteller. It was a truly unique exposition—sultry without being sordid. However, no wonder the book was anonymous—if word got out, she would be utterly ruined. Other writers who had penned books with suggestive matter had been condemned and shunned for immorality, even imprisoned, their work deemed depraved and obscene. Both men and women, though in their world, women had much more to lose.

Jasper frowned, a thought occurring to him, as his eyes darted from the book in his hand to the parchment that had been sent to Briar, still sitting on the corner of his desk.

I know your secret. I have my eyes on you, little dove.

His stomach dipped, arousal dissolving as dread lodged

itself deep. What if whoever had sent her the message didn't mean her visits to Lethe? What if they meant *this*? Her secret and very scandalous vocation. That would change everything.

Because the first was salvageable; the second would be her utter ruin.

With a curse, Briar crumpled the parchment and sighed at the ink she'd gotten all over her fingers. It was official—her muse was on hiatus. Her imagination, formerly so fertile, was now barren, and she had a sneaking suspicion it had to do with her fictional engagement to a certain gentleman. Because all she could think about was *him*.

As much as he *had* loosely inspired some of her heroes— she made it a point to give some of them dark or light hair with brown or green eyes—she couldn't very well describe a living person. Someone in her very discerning group of friends might make the connection. They already read her stories and would take her secret to the grave, but they *knew* Lushing. Her best friend was the man's sister! She doubted Vesper would appreciate *any* correlation between her brother and an amorous lover begging to be flogged.

Pressing her knuckles to her flushed cheeks, Briar let out a hysterical giggle.

Her brain was obsessed with hair shades of copper, strawberry, and garnet...and eyes that ran from sapphire to cerulean, nothing so humdrum as blue. And the thought of even writing the earl into fiction—describing that athletic, vigorous body without a shred of clothing, while restraining

Lady Ivy with her wrists pinned and her body folded over a cleverly designed piece of furniture—drenched her drawers every time.

Theresa Berkley might be long dead, but her genius lived on. Heat exploded in Briar's stomach at the thought of the infamous Berkley Horse that she'd meticulously researched and reinvented. The last volume of Lady Ivy's adventures had been a runaway success with readers already clamoring for the next installment.

She'd already received a slew of fervent letters from her printer and bookseller, Theophilus Judge, with promises of more printed copies and higher profit shares. He owned C. Brown, a smaller publisher of subversive literature.

At first, her agreement with Theo had only been for printing. But when the initial fifty copies flew off the press like hotcakes, he proposed a new agreement. Theo was young, barely twenty-eight, to her own twenty-one. He was the only one who knew that she was a woman—though she kept her face hidden—and as long as they were in the business of making money, he would not jeopardize a solid source of income.

She'd asked Theo once why he published such literature, including hers, that could send him to prison for obscenity, and he'd responded that happiness was rare enough. Who was he to judge what a person could read? As long as it wasn't hurting anyone, it was none of his business.

The reasoning had stuck with her.

In a time when morality and virtue overshadowed everything, writing her stories, prurient as they were, was liberating. Since women's bodies were treated like property, there was little thought given to their needs, especially sexual ones. But women were not receptacles—they were active participants. *Partners.* Everyone should be able to find joy in their own bodies without being shamed for it.

When and why had pleasure become a crime of immorality?

Briar scowled. As Mary Wollstonecraft had written three-quarters of a century ago, women were not a fanciful kind of half being, nor were they useless members of society—they should be educated and given the same rights as men. Women deserved autonomy over their own bodies and their own minds. They deserved the right to vote. It was no surprise that her suffrage interests intersected with her erotic works. Political change went hand-in-hand with sexual freedom.

"Briar, darling, are you at home to callers?"

She grinned when Laila and Effie crowded her study.

"Oh, are you writing a new volume?" Effie practically screeched and fanned herself, proceeding to collapse into an armchair. "The last was simply *delectable.* Honestly, I'm not even into being birched, and I asked Vale to find some, post haste. Your writing makes me want to ask for all the things without an ounce of shame!"

"That's the goal," Briar said, peering at Laila who was scarlet with mortification and hiding her face. "Not to your liking, then, Laila? I admit caning is not for everyone. I was intrigued by the idea of pleasure and pain, after hearing about it from one of the ladies at Lethe, and I fell down a rabbit hole that was rather illuminating."

"No, on the contrary, I was fascinated," Laila squeaked, going redder. "Turns out, I enjoy it. Though...with his h... hand, not a switch."

Effie's eyes went wide. "Laila, you naughty little minx! Tell us more."

Looking as though she was about to burst, Laila bit her lip. "Truly, it was life altering. I haven't experienced such a powerful orgasm ever."

"Did Marsden provide the appropriate care afterward?" Briar asked. "These things can be very intense, so the circle has to be closed, so to speak."

"He did," she said. "I loved how well you explained that. I must admit, it fostered a deeper connection between us that I never expected." She cleared her throat and pressed her knuckles to her hot cheeks. "I know that you and Effie are far more adventurous than I am, but well, thank you for expressing it in such a beautiful and thoughtful way, especially for a novice."

"You're welcome," Briar said, flushing with pleasure at the quiet praise. Her books might be viewed as salacious, but stories were complex. For one reader, her books could be an escape, and for another, they could be instructive or inspirational. Stories were doorways—where they took a person was entirely up to them.

"She's right!" Effie agreed. "Your ability to make the profane so remarkably poetic is unrivaled."

"Thank you, Effie," Briar said. "Though my muse seems to have disappeared."

"Is it because you're a taken woman?" Effie teased, and Briar shot Laila an accusing glare.

"Don't look at me!" Laila said, throwing her palms up. "The newspapers and the gossip rags were already agog with speculation. And after last night's ball when you danced *five* times with Lushing, your fate was sealed. Everyone either expects it or claims your engagement has already happened."

"So, are you truly engaged?" Effie asked.

Briar nodded and pinned her lips, hating the fact that she had to lie to her best friends. Then again, Effie hadn't been forthcoming with her lessons in sensual pleasure with her duke, and Nève hadn't told anyone about her paid contract with Montcroix. Vesper probably had more skeletons than all of them put together hidden in the cupboard. Only Laila seemed to be exempt, and that was probably because she was the best secret-keeper of them all. The woman was a vault.

Effie's brows lifted. "And you're certain that Lushing is the one? Everyone knows I adore the gingery rapscallion, but it's *Lushing*. Put the two of you in a room, and it's anyone's best bet who comes out alive. My money is on you, of course."

Briar was getting tired of the way everyone said his name, as though he were some kind of wretched anomaly. "Yes, I've heard it all from Laila, don't worry," she replied. "Look, I know what everyone thinks. But we've become... friends."

"You hesitated! Say that to my face!" Effie shot back.

Briar peered into Effie's ice-blue eyes, making hers comically round for emphasis. "The Earl of Lushing and I are friends. Happy now?" She sighed. "Bloody hell, why is that so hard to believe?"

"I don't know, Briar, maybe the years and years of bickering and backbiting. Maybe wondering which one of you was going to do away with the other first. Maybe because you've been enemies for practically *forever*."

"It's a prologue," Laila said, and both women stared nonplussed at her. She shrugged. "One leading to a buildup of, in plain terms, lust. Enemies who become lovers!"

"No one is becoming anything, and I am *not* lusting after the man," Briar protested and then shoved Effie away, who was attempting once more to peer into her soul to gauge her sincerity. Her ears felt absurdly hot, and she was worried her face would follow. "This shall be a marriage of convenience, nothing more. Like many others in the aristocracy."

"Lushing does nothing out of convenience," Effie quipped. "He's quite easy on the eyes, you have to admit that." She grinned wickedly, waggling her pale blond brows. "In fact, the hero in Volume Two of Lady Ivy's grand adventures, the dashing young painter who painted her nude portrait, seemed to have an uncanny resemblance to a certain gent, if I reca—"

A cushion to the face had her words ending abruptly. Hair askew, Effie gaped in outrage. "I've at least three cushions here," Briar warned, holding a second aloft. "The painter's hair was reddish *brown*. His eyes were bluish *green*."

Effie opened her mouth to argue and closed it as Briar hefted a cushion in preparation, but it was Laila who intervened by deftly changing the subject. "I am curious as to why you believe your muse has deserted you?"

Briar couldn't very well say a blue-eyed, redheaded gentleman *now*.

"I suppose I'm being pulled in two directions. Katherine, er, Viscountess Amberley has asked me to draft a new petition for the next suffragist meeting. Her focus is elsewhere because her husband is addressing the London Dialectical Society on voluntary reproductive control, which as you can imagine is deeply controversial. Because why should women possibly want to safeguard their own wombs and bodies?" She didn't curb her sarcasm as her friends huffed in unison. "I need to convey how important suffrage is to our members."

Both women immediately grew serious. "How can we help?"

The little harpy was marauding the streets again. Though this time she wasn't looking for men mistreating women in Seven Dials. Jasper had followed her to Whitechapel in East London. He strode over to where the loyal Olsen was waiting with her unmarked carriage some distance away. Jasper sent the man a quick signal that he would take over and watched when the coachman tipped his hat and took his leave. Like other times, he knew that Jasper would see Briar safely home.

Jasper narrowed his gaze on the meeting that was occurring inside the tavern through the cloudy windows. It appeared to be a meeting of the suffragists, if only from recognizing Lady Amberley and Millicent Fawcett, who were part of the executive committee of the London National Society for Women's Suffrage.

Pulling his cloak hood low, he entered through the back of the tavern and found a darkened corner, out of sight of the main room. His view was partially obscured by the wide slats in the half wall, but he could hear the discussion clearly. The women spoke in low voices as the tavern was not closed for business, but it was out of the way enough to not draw the wrong kind of attention.

Jasper canvassed the score or so of determined faces from the aristocracy and the gentry. Bloody hell, some of the women were so young. He knew for a fact that Millicent was barely twenty, though she was married to a Cambridge University professor. Lady Katherine Russell, Viscountess Amberley was twenty-five or thereabouts, and Briar, still unwed, was twenty-one. He knew their youth was deceptive, however. These women might be young, but they were forces of nature.

He also recognized his family's—and Lethe's—physician, Dr. Elizabeth Garrett, a titan in her own right, who had earned her certificate as a doctor and established a dispensary for women two years ago. She was also Millicent's eldest sister, so it was no surprise that she was there. The intelligence and ambition in that one room alone could destroy and lead whole empires. Jasper had no doubt that they would be successful in winning the right to vote someday.

In truth, he was in vehement support of it. Women deserved the same rights as men. Especially the women who gave voices to those who had none. Like the one woman he could not keep his eye off. Briar Fairview was beautiful and made even more so by that stunningly brilliant mind.

Some men were intimidated by smart women. Not him. Jasper loved pitting himself against her intelligence and witnessing that razor-sharp wit at work. She had cut him down to size many-a-time with a few choice words, but more than that, she never failed to impress him.

She'd astounded him with the women at Lethe, fighting for their right to live and prosper, despite how society viewed their choices. She'd dazzled him with her evocative writing and her unflinching pursuit of female pleasure.

And she captivated him now, standing toe-to-toe with some of the greatest minds in England. Her intense expression was unwavering as she listened to something Millicent was saying before taking the floor. Jasper caught his breath.

Briar stood and cleared her throat, holding up a piece of paper as she read, "It has long been our role that a woman's place is in the home with the duties of wife and mother. But I ask you now, ladies, lords, and gentlemen, how can we fulfill our full potential and pursue our duties without the same education and political freedoms as our husbands?" The women broke out in claps and cheers, and Jasper was utterly entranced. He'd never seen her like this—a persuasive, visionary leader. "We are bound by laws, without having a voice. Our bodies are not our own, as though we require permission to exist or to thrive. We are taxed, while we are considered property. Any wealth we acquire or inherit is given to our husbands. Upon marriage, we have no rights, own no land, and have no say. Is this just, I ask you?"

"No!" the women chorused, and Briar smiled.

Christ, Jasper could not stop staring at her. Her eyes glowed with passion, her color high, making her skin luminous in the lamplight. "Politics are not for men alone. Our brains are just as capable"—she grinned with a saucy wink that arrowed straight to his groin—"or, dare I say, even more so than men. Do we not shape the minds of our children? Share the burdens of our spouses? Are we not half of the citizens of this great nation? Then why should we not have the vote?"

More cheers ensued, even a few whistles.

She set down the paper, meeting the eye of everyone in the room with the skill of a great orator. "We are *partners* in the joint endeavors of marriage and companionship, consummation and parenthood. We stand stronger together, not apart. Men, women, or any adult with a voice should be heard. I urge you to sign our petition so we may go before Parliament and seek reform, so we may celebrate the fruit of true partnership and a united future."

"Hear, hear!" several voices called out.

Jasper exhaled in absolute wonder, shaking his head and clapping with the others. He must have made a noise or done something because her head swiveled, eyes slamming into where he sat, though he was still obscured by shadow. Her gaze sharpened but then slid away as she took her seat. Jasper waited until the meeting adjourned, watching as everyone dissipated until only Briar, Millicent, Elizabeth, and the viscountess were left.

"Do you require transportation, Lady Briar?" one of the women asked.

She shook her head, curls bouncing. "No, thank you. My coachman is just outside."

"See you next week. Thank you for your wonderful work tonight."

Briar flushed with pride. Jasper smiled. She *should* be proud—she was magnificent.

He followed her in silence, watching as she tugged a deep cowl over her head and obscured her features before exiting. She was careful to walk briskly along the well-lit street, her gait sure and her presence confident to deter any cutpurses who might assume wrongly that she was a weak mark. But if they did, he knew that she would be armed. He snorted under his breath. Fearless to a fault.

Jasper waited until she stopped, frowning at the spot where her carriage should have been before peering up and down the street. Then he pounced, herding her into a nearby alley and narrowly avoiding a fist to his face as well as a vicious knee to the groin. He couldn't fully avoid the knuckles that came for his jaw, however, or the switchblade that pressed into his jugular. Damn, she was fast.

"Hullo, Sweetbriar," he said.

"Jasper," she gasped, instantly ceasing her attack. Fuck, he loved the sound of his name on her lips. "I could have killed you, you sapscull!" She glowered at him. "I knew I sensed you in the tavern."

Smirking, he lifted a brow. "You *sensed* me?"

"Like a hundred spiders crawling on my skin," she said, scowl darkening. "Like a plague of festering boils. Like explosive diarrhea."

"Lying isn't a good look on you, Prickles." He pinned her against the brick with his hips, a gasp flying from her lips at what she undoubtedly felt, even beneath all her skirts. He'd been rock-hard since she'd started speaking in the tavern. Lightning fast, he knocked the blade out of her hand and gripped her wrist. When she attempted to punch him with her free hand, he ducked and grasped that too, securing them both above her head.

It was a position she'd written, not that she would guess *he* knew.

But in the guttered streetlight, her lips parted, and her pupils dilated. Good...she *liked* being helpless, even though she could escape his hold, if she truly wanted to. He waited, just in case his instincts were wrong, but her breaths became shallower and shallower as she stayed rooted in place, her eyes huge.

"Some men like a beautiful face, others prefer a shapely body, but that stunningly erudite brain of yours, Sweetbriar, is its own wicked seduction." He buried his nose in her fragrant hair and inhaled deeply. "And I swear that it has ruined me. You were outstanding tonight. Truly, if you could speak directly to Parliament, women would have the vote tomorrow. After all, how could anyone hope to withstand the storm that is Briar Fairview?"

Her eyelids fluttered and then went wide as she tried to see around him, yanking her arms down in confusion. "Wait. Is this...are we...pretending? Are one of the ladies close by?"

"No."

She blinked, an adorable furrow appearing between her brows. "Then what...why are you doing this?"

"Because I *need* to fucking kiss you."

"Oh," she breathed.

He waited again for tacit permission, and when she melted against him, her free hands curling into his lapels with a yearning that matched his, he finally claimed the lips that had taunted him for fucking *years*.

There was softness, but only at first. Her lips parted, and he accepted the invitation, his tongue sliding tentatively across her lower lip. Jasper groaned at the sweetness, need crashing through his veins so violently that he shook from the force of it. He wanted to be gentle, to make it tender, but she wouldn't let him, growling in her throat and nipping at his mouth. She yanked him closer, teeth grazing his lips, the aggression like flame to tinder.

"Kiss me back, damn it," she commanded, and Jasper felt something inside of him crack.

He fell upon her like an animal, moaning at the sublime feel of her as his tongue plunged deep to tangle with hers. Fuck, she tasted like heaven and sin wrapped in one. Tart, sweet, deadly. One hand wound into the mass of hair at her nape and tightened into a fist as he drew her head back, feasting on that luscious mouth and clever tongue, while the other grasped her arse and dragged her lower half into his.

Lust ripped through him when she bit his lower lip and sucked hard as if he wasn't the only one who could make carnal demands. He smiled against her mouth as she took and he gave, and then the dance reversed. He left no part of that lush, smart mouth unexplored, dragged his tongue down her throat and back up, savoring the frantic flutter of her pulse at the base of her neck and every delectable inch before claiming those plump lips again. He couldn't get enough. Never enough.

It felt as though they kissed for hours before he pulled away, panting. "Briar..."

Her green eyes were blown with desire, her lips swollen and bruised as she stared at him in stricken silence. He felt the same...utterly thunderstruck.

"*More.*"

CHAPTER SEVEN

The four other members of the Hellfire Kitties stared at her over the tea table with varying degrees of disbelief, wonder, and I-told-you-so satisfaction, the last of course from Vesper, who couldn't stop preening over her incomparable match-making brilliance. She was, in true Vesper fashion, taking all the credit, though Briar didn't mind. Her friend deserved whatever joy she could get.

"I knew you would be perfect for each other!" she crowed. "I told him to get off his arse and strike while the iron was hot."

"Didn't you hear what I said? It's not real," Briar said, sipping her tea and nearly scalding her tongue. She'd sent a message to the earl that she could no longer keep the truth from her friends. To her surprise, he had agreed, and so, here she was. "This farce is simply a means to an end."

A means to an end that was becoming more treacherous by the day.

Because by God, that *kiss*.

It was as though it had been brewing for an eternity,

building and building into something so explosive that stars had fallen from their orbit. Or at least, it had felt that way. Like everything in the cosmos had been inexplicably altered. *She* had been changed down to her cellular matter. After she had shamelessly begged for more, her entire body on fire, Lushing had obliged until they had both almost dissolved into a tangled coil of heat, lust, and shivering desire.

And then they'd both sworn never to do it again.

Though every single hour of the day since, she *yearned* for his touch. Briar had experimented with kissing before, but *none* of them had been like that. Cataclysmic and all-consuming. Her mind had been inventive with her writing, but her body had never made the connection between what she wrote and what she felt.

Certainly, she'd experienced the sparks of arousal. But *that single kiss* had turned her arousal into an inferno, and now that her senses were awakened, it was all she could do to not show up at the earl's residence with nothing but a cloak, a crop, and a pair of boots, and demand he finish what he started.

Which was *never* going to happen.

Because everything was going perfectly to plan, and if they were lucky, they would each get what they hoped for— their former partners. Briar was stunned at how quickly their artifice had worked. Given that the *ton* loved gossip, when they had first appeared together as a couple at the opera a fortnight ago, the tongues had wagged nonstop about whether they'd been secretly courting all along, something that everyone had allegedly long suspected.

A load of poppycock, of course.

High society loved nothing more than drama and

amorous intrigues. As predicted, Viscount Sackley seemed to be regretting his hasty rejection, particularly when the denizens of the *ton* raved about Lady Briar's brave and charitable endeavors, and her decidedly *virtuous* nature. That was mostly thanks to her mother's connections with all the influential dowagers. Briar leaned into the praise with everything she had, swiftly becoming the new darling of the *ton*.

And likewise, the perfect Lady Penelope had become rather prickly, sending longing glances toward the Earl of Lushing whenever they were at the same social events, which was often by design. The lady, too, was bemoaning her injudicious acceptance of the suit of a man who was considerably less *everything* than the dashing earl.

Less titled, less rich, less charming, less handsome...

Briar didn't miss the jealous looks she received, which her dreadful self-absorbed cohort seemed to love leaning into as well. This was more than a matter of pride to him. He wanted Penelope *crawling* as he'd admitted to Briar. She had yet to reconcile how the growled confession had seeped into her bones like oil over gravel, making the slumbering beast inside lift its head with coy interest. Given the chance, *she* would yield at a simple command from him. Briar would crawl on her hands and knees if he told her to.

Even now, she wanted to squirm in her garden chair.

Briar firmed her lips and focused on the matter at hand, her *friends* and not the fantasies of her wanton inner self. "My precious darlings, what you've seen over the past two weeks has been crafty subterfuge. I assure you, Lushing is not interested in me, nor the reverse."

Vesper let out a vulgar scoff of amusement as Effie pinned her lips to keep from likely doing the same. Both

Nève and Laila feigned deep interest in their scones, their expressions of disbelief nearly identical.

"Could have fooled me," someone muttered. It sounded like Effie, the wretch.

Briar sighed and reached for patience. "We are simply doing what we must to convince our former paramours of their mistakes," she explained.

She knew that her friends had always insisted there was something between Lushing and her...but that something was reciprocated antagonism. Attraction notwithstanding, they were like chalk and cheese with nothing in common beyond their wonderful mutual circle of friends. Briar still found the earl infuriatingly arrogant; he still found her tiresomely stubborn. They were both too competitive and controlling to bend to the other.

Maybe not in bed...

Goodness, where had *that* thought come from?

Heat flooded her cheeks as the visceral memory of his hard body in that alleyway and the way he'd grasped her hair in his tight fist rose up to taunt her. When he'd held her close, she had felt the wide breadth of his chest against her, the length of his muscled thighs, and *that* part of him. The hard ridge against her belly had felt quite sizable.

The women at Lethe talked, and the Earl of Lushing wasn't lacking in anything—property or prowess. Though he didn't make a habit of bedding women at his own establishment, juicy gossip found its way between streets and station, and such gossip usually included tidbits about Lethe's much-too-attractive and exceedingly virile owner.

For the love of God, stop thinking about him or his deuced virility.

Briar glanced at her friends. "Can we talk about something else now?"

"But nothing else is as exciting," Vesper said with a pout.

"This is. Do any of you have ideas for Lady Ivy?" she asked, keeping her voice low. Her identity was still a closely guarded secret after all, and it only took one slip in front of the servants for the truth to get out. "After the last volume, I'm afraid I've hit a wall. Apparently, my muse has decided to go on hiatus."

They all perked up after that as Briar reached for the small notebook in her reticule to jot down any notes.

"So, this past volume was flogging," Nève said. "With the special furniture in the flagellation room, yes? Excellent work, by the way. I enjoyed the story, even though it's not really my cup of tea." She shook her head with a small wince. "Considering the physical torture I endured with my ruined toes for ballet, the idea of pain doesn't seem very pleasurable."

"Thank you for saying that," Briar said softly. "I'm so sorry about your suffering. That's the beauty of books— there's something for everyone. I want to cover a wide range of study for my readers to feel comfortable with their likes and dislikes."

"Each to their own," Effie chimed in. "I don't mind a good swat, and Laila *loves* it."

A cushion flew at her face, and everyone giggled. "I do," Laila admitted and ducked her head. "Wait, the flagellation room. Is *that* what it's called?"

Nève grinned. "She is a special *governess*, Laila. She must discipline her naughty lovers somewhere." She held up a finger to her chin. "If I recall, the book before that was the visit to one of the most elite brothels in Paris, *La Fleur Blanche,* and the infamous coitus chair."

Biting her lip, Briar nodded. "That was a fantastic suggestion. Who knew carpenters could be so ingenious?"

"That French count was rather inventive and adventurous with the seat," Effie said. "Especially when he took it into the garden with Lady Ivy *and* the courtesan."

Everyone twittered, hands rising to suddenly flushed cheeks.

"I love a good, luxurious bed," Nève said. "I do not see the lure of a lack of comfort. I adore indulgence too much."

"One does have to be resourceful," Effie mused. "I admit Vale and I rarely make it to a bed. The uses of furniture can be quite versatile. We even tried a valet's stand and a vanity once. It's remarkable what the right height can do, especially when one's head is hanging over the side, and his phallus, er, well, never mind..."

"Effie!" Nève whisper-screamed under her breath.

Effie rolled her eyes. "I don't know what you're pretending to be so scandalized about—you're the one with the flexibility to do ballet splits during copulation. Anyone with abnormal joints can sit down."

"That was a secret!" she hissed.

Briar grinned. "One that appeared in volume number three, might I remind you, with the voyeuristic show at the theater."

They burst into giggles as Laila pointed a finger at Vesper. "I don't know why Cupidella is being so quiet over there, knowing she and her fondness for outdoor adventures inspired volume number four. I shall never be able to visit the Crystal Palace again without being properly horrified at the indignities those poor statues suffered."

Vesper pinned her lips with a snort, but a look of odd melancholy stole over her features that she tried to hide without much success.

Noticing her swift change in mood, Briar frowned. "Are you well, Ves?"

Her friend's throat worked as everyone quieted. "Aspen and I haven't had done much of anything in a while. I worry things will never return to the way they were. Audra is thriving now, and he's been so patient with me. I fear he'll leave me." A lone tear tracked down her face. "I can't lose him."

"Greydon loves you, Vesper," Laila interjected softly. "He's not going anywhere. As a mother myself, it took a while for intimacy to resume with us after our son, but it will. You must allow your body *and* your mind some grace. You went through an ordeal."

"Can you go somewhere alone for a few days?" Effie suggested. "Audra has a nurse, no? You've been weaning her off the breast?"

"Yes," Vesper whispered. "But I'm not sure I should leave. Doesn't that make me a terrible mother, if I do?"

"You can't look after anyone else if you don't look after yourself, Vesper," Nève said firmly. "Lysander and I had to take some time to reconnect after Philippe's birth. It doesn't make you a bad parent, it makes you a healthier wife and mother."

"They're right," Briar said. "A short holiday might help. Why don't you take a few days and go to Bath? There's no one at our house there and we're very close to the water.

Think of all the statues you and Greydon can desecrate in my poor garden."

A watery smile broke over Vesper's face, though she still seemed unsure.

"I can look after Audra for you," Laila volunteered. "And Briar can supply all the lewd reading materials to get you and your bone-master in the mood." Vesper's eyes widened as she stifled a giggle. It was no secret that the Duke of Greydon was an avid paleontologist, which had led to a whole host of humorous and very bawdy puns. "I can attest that congress in the water is...highly underrated," Laila added with a small cough.

"Truly?" Effie exclaimed, pale blue eyes rounding. "In the *ocean?*"

Laila blushed. "Think of it as just a bigger bath...with people around as well as being wildly creative with swimming costumes."

"You little deviant," Effie said as Briar wrote furiously in her notebook.

"Let's not mock each other's preferences or fetishes, Effie dear," Laila shot back with a saccharine look, wiggling her eyebrows. "People in glass houses should not throw stones... or dildos."

After a protracted moment, everyone broke into raucous cackles, so much so that the servant bringing in a fresh pot of tea turned instantly on her heel and disappeared. The poor maids and footmen had been scandalized enough over the years.

"She has you there, Effie," Nève said, gasping for breath.

"Dildos are a person's best friends," Effie said sagely. "And don't knock self-pleasure—have you seen some of the new designs? Some of them have channels and springs for hot oil or milk. Of all the things, that has to be the most curious."

"Truly fascinating," Nève put in. "The French are absurdly ingenious, especially when it comes to sexual contraptions mimicking the real thing."

Unlike her friends, who were all married and clearly living enviable and satisfied personal lives, Briar was still a virgin. It wasn't that she wasn't interested or saving herself for marriage—if a man could sow his wild oats, then why shouldn't a woman be able to do the same? She simply had never found anyone she could trust with herself—and her very peculiar intimate fantasies. Books and her stories had become a safe space where she could discover and see herself on the page. At first, she'd started reading them, and then she'd begun *crafting* them.

Living vicariously and boldly through the dauntless Lady Ivy, who wasn't afraid to admit she loved bondage, power reversals, or being degraded and praised, was the best option for her. Especially if she eventually married someone like the viscount.

Divulging those appetites in real life required a deep amount of trust with one's partner, and without a doubt, Preston would sooner lock her up in a lunatic asylum for hysteria than praise her prowess in the bedroom. The man did not have a passionate bone in his body.

She reminded herself that she only needed him for the use of his name. She had Lady Ivy, and that was good enough for her.

"All of this, including perhaps a visit to the French seaside and experimentation with pleasure toys, is gold,"

Briar said, her pencil scribbling on the paper as she jotted down a few more ideas. "I swear Lady Ivy is an amalgamation of all of us."

Nève cleared her throat, pursing her lips and glancing around. "If that's the case, which one of us is the one who loves being made to crawl and called a good girl?"

"Uh..." There was no judgment in the amused inquiry, but Briar's face exploded as though it was on literal fire. Thankfully, given the conversation, everyone was flushed. She forced herself to give a casual shrug, keeping her expression as neutral as possible. "Minthe."

"*Minthe*," Effie bit out ferociously. She'd always thought that Minthe had had a secret infatuation with her husband before the two of them had declared their feelings for each other. Vale, of course, only had eyes for Effie, but the beautiful bookkeeper remained a sore spot for her. Vulnerability was a devil of a thing. "Honestly, how can you not worry that Lushing is working with her all day, Briar? She's terribly flirtatious."

"Minthe is more interested in *me* than him," she replied with a laugh.

"And the only person my brother esteems is himself," Vesper said and then winked, her good humor back again. "Unless it's Briar, of course. Let it be said that I predict a wedding date between the prickliest pair in London by the end of the season. Shall we toast for good luck? To the last bride!"

"The last bride!" the rest cheered, lifting their teacups and making Briar scowl.

She did not want to think about marrying the Earl of

Lushing...or what being his wife would entail. No, their collaboration would remain amicable and platonic. Chaste.

Nothing about that kiss was chaste.

Her brain was much too preoccupied with the delicious taste of him, the divine scent of him, and the rough sound of his groans when he kissed her as if he couldn't get enough. Her core gave an indelicate ripple that almost made her lose her breath.

No, no, no. That was a very slippery slope, and one she had to avoid at all costs.

"Fine," she shouted over the noise. "But my wedding will be to *Viscount Sackley*, not Lord Lushing. That is the whole point of the endeavor. Calm yourselves!"

"Boooooo!" The chorus was enthusiastic and loud enough for Briar to clap her hands over her ears as they all dissolved into another round of boisterous laughter, causing the servants to peek out at the ensuing chaos.

Then again, some kind of chaos was naturally expected when they were all together. Briar couldn't help smiling at her rowdy, brilliant, and faithful friends. They would always be there, through thick and thin.

Hellfire Kitties forever.

Jasper tugged at his cuffs and straightened his cravat while he was waiting for Briar to arrive at the Duke and Duchess of Montcroix's residence for the most anticipated mid-season ball. Earlier that afternoon, she had been meeting with her brother Levi. Another letter had arrived, this one much darker in nature, and they had immediately contacted the

Metropolitan Police. One note was concerning, a second made it a possible pattern.

And this one had been worse than the first: *You stray from the path with corrupt passions, but don't fear, little dove, you are mine to save. Soon.*

Briar still had no idea who it could be, but the threat was obvious.

Jasper had been disinclined to go to the ball, but she had insisted on attending, certain that this particular ball would be pivotal in their combined efforts. She wasn't wrong. Their performance was almost ending. Penelope had already called at his residence, asking for an audience. Jasper had refused.

The truth was, he wasn't ready for their fake engagement to end just yet.

He couldn't wait to have Briar on his arm, even if it was for one last time. He wasn't quite sure when the pleasure had switched to the delight of being in her presence instead of seeing the reactions of their former partners. He and Briar had been at odds for so long that conspiring together against the world felt oddly exhilarating.

It felt *right* in a way that could not be explained.

Even at Lethe, they were a cohesive pair. Whether that was a result of their increased proximity, he didn't know, but the club had never been better. Her brilliant ideas of hiring a French chef and purchasing the rest of the building to include a library and several apartments had doubled the profit of the club and more than paid for the initial outlay of funds. As a partner in business, he could not have been more fortunate. She was canny, forward-thinking, and shrewd with money. Sharper than most men, including him.

"My lord, don't you look dashing!" Her voice curled around him just before her sultry night-blooming jasmine scent did.

He jerked and stared, jaw going slack. Powder blue wasn't a color one would call seductive; at best, it looked nice. It wasn't a bold hue like the crimson she'd worn to the opera. But Briar—*Christ*—she looked like a vision of innocence wrapped in pure sin. It was the Grecian style that left one bronze shoulder tantalizingly visible, combined with the delicate color of the fabric. The contradiction left him breathless.

The soft blue was just the right hue to make her mouthwatering skin glow and brought out the amber and chartreuse flecks in her eyes. Her brown spirals were lustrous and glossy, kissing the long column of her throat and exposed shoulder. There was nothing *nice* about the slanted bodice that clung to her curves, or the way the ripples of silk molded to her cinched waist and voluptuously flared hips. His mouth was so dry, he could barely fucking speak.

"You look stunning," he said and then cleared his throat when his voice emerged in an unnatural croak. "One of the marchioness's creations, I presume?"

"Thank you, Lord Lushing. And yes, Laila is indeed a marvel." Her eyes narrowed for a beat at his clearly besotted expression before she canted her head and lowered her voice to a conspiratorial level. "Is complimenting each other like this part of our performance? Are Sackley and Penelope here already?"

"Not that I can see," he said, frowning slightly. "Can't a man simply be smitten by a beautiful woman?"

Flags of color lit her cheeks, but she didn't respond to his question, as if determined to keep things cool and distant between them. "We should dance while we can. The more we're seen, the better off we will be. Penelope's mother let it slip to mine that her daughter might have made a terrible mistake. Whenever I'm in your arms, she's green with envy." Briar's brows pinched. "So, our plan is working better than we hoped. Soon, you will have exactly what you wanted...for her to come crawling back."

He jolted. It wasn't *Penelope* he was suddenly imagining on her hands and knees. What if what he wanted wasn't the same anymore?

The question came out of nowhere.

"As will you." Jasper extended his elbow, which she took, and he escorted her to the circle of dancers. To his surprise, Sackley and Penelope were both paired up as well. Jasper lowered his head, bussing his lips over Briar's gloved knuckles. "They're here."

Briar craned her head immediately. "Where?"

"About to dance."

Her mouth curled down at the sight of the couple. "But he hates dancing!"

"Perhaps they are hoping to beat us at our own game," Jasper said as he slid his fingers over her waist and grasped her free palm with his own. "We have been doing a marvelous job of seeming deliriously happy."

"Have we?" she murmured, distracted and equally dismayed.

"Eyes on me, Briar," he said with a low rumble of command in his tone, one that had her entire body going as taut as a bowstring. Her attention immediately flicked to him, those green irises bright with instant lust. When hot splotches of crimson flooded her cheeks, he smirked. So, she *hadn't* forgotten what that kiss had felt like.

Well, neither had he.

Jasper hoarded her unguarded reaction, solidifying his suspicion that his sneaky little storyteller *loved* being told what to do. He would not have predicted that without having read her book, though it made sense. Powerful women sometimes had submissive urges, especially in the bedchamber. And she'd practically written out a wish list with Lady Ivy. His blood heated. A wish list *he* was suddenly desperate to deliver.

"Don't tell me what to do," she belatedly snapped, though the slightest tremor in her words gave her away.

"Prickles, what have I said?" he murmured, expertly guiding her into the first turn. "Lie to everyone else but not to me." He leaned in, voice pitched low and deep, fingers dancing over the curve of her hip. "Secretly, somewhere deep down inside"—he kneaded his fingers into her flesh and changed the cadence of his tone to something far more intimate—"you're *fascinated* by the idea of someone ordering you about because you *want* nothing more than to give up control."

The shudder beneath her skin and the increased pace of her breaths were the only indications she had heard him. It was a true credit to her poise that her face remained neutral despite its heightened color and that her feet obediently mimicked his for each beat of the waltz.

His voice dropped to gravel. "You *crave* being instructed on what to do, don't you?"

The pulse at the base of her neck throbbed wildly, and he

longed to collar that beautiful throat and trace his thumb over that spot...press his tongue to it and make that fluttering pulse go wild. As it had in the alley in Whitechapel. Jasper licked his lips instead, watching her passion-blown eyes dip to his mouth, her own lips parting on a needy sigh.

Bloody hell, if they weren't in a public ballroom, he'd kiss her senseless.

His thumb grazed over the inside of her wrist, making her quiver. "Did you know there are rooms at Lethe that allow for the safe, consensual exploration of certain appetites?"

The question detonated like a bomb between them. Those beautiful eyes hunted his as if looking for the censure that would certainly come. It would not. He would never make her feel ashamed of her desires, but that would take time...and trust. God, he *wanted* her to trust him. Needed it like his next breath. Though that was the thing with trust— it had to be earned.

Finally, she found her voice, which was huskier than usual. "I have no idea what you're talking about, Lord Lushing. Yes, I am aware that you have an exceptional restaurant at Lethe to satisfy even the most discerning of *appetites*."

He hid his grin at her deflection.

"There you go, lying again," he whispered, twirling her once more so that their path neared the couple they were meant to be inciting.

"I am not," she said primly.

"Minthe is reportedly exceptional at flagellation," he went on, reveling in the tiny stumble before she righted herself. "Has she ever told you that she does it on a whim from time to time at Lethe? Some of the members revere her skills."

He wound his fingers wickedly into the pleated fabric at her waist, pulling the delicate silk taut against her skin. Her sharp intake of breath was a delight to his senses. *How* had he not known that outspoken, brash, independent Lady Briar Fairview had such singular desires...ones that *he* was perfectly equipped to tantalize and satiate?

"Why are you telling me this?" she asked.

"Because she's a fascinating woman."

"I'll be sure to let her know of your interest," she tossed back as green eyes slammed into his, brightening with something other than lust before it was throttled away.

"Trust me, Sweetbriar, she's not who I want."

His companion huffed. "Goodness, Lord Lushing, you change your mind like a high society lady changes garments. First Penelope, then Minthe. Who will you want tomorrow?"

"I only want one woman." He leaned in, mouth grazing her ear as they spun. "And she's a willful brat who needs to know her place."

She fumbled her steps, nearly causing a collision, and then did the unimaginable: she left him right there in the middle of the ballroom floor. The whispers reached the rafters, other dancers craning their necks to see what the fuss was. A chuckling Jasper didn't care. She was a fucking goddess who could do whatever she wanted, everyone else be damned.

By God, he wanted to demolish every single one of her inhibitions, but the armor she wore was near impenetrable. He wanted to be the one to see her bloom and take her pleasure without any shame, or worse, any fear of being judged. That was the problem with society in general—all the fucking rules they had as to one's private identity.

What did it matter when desire and love were both fluid things that could exist separately and in tandem? How did the events of the bedchamber or elsewhere between consenting adults impact the very fabric of moral society? It was ludicrous. Sexual congress was natural and healthy. Procreation and the continuation of humanity was simply *one* outcome. Pleasure was another. The doctrine that women should shy away from pleasure to control brittle male impulses had always been laughable to him. Women weren't responsible for the actions of men.

Their hushed conversation while waltzing scandalously close had already garnered attention. The lady's outrageous, indecorous exit in the middle of a dance, even more so. And not only from the surrounding spectators whose tongues were already wagging with censorious glee. Jasper could feel the probing stares from both the viscount and his fiancée.

He'd never, *ever* leave her to the wolves, so he prowled after her to where she stood on the terrace, gripping the balustrade and hauling deep breaths into her lungs.

"Go away, Lushing," she said, but she didn't sound upset. She was *breathless*.

"I'll have to punish you for that, you know, storming off without *permission*," he drawled, joining her where she stood and noting her shiver with a satisfied smile. "Perhaps I'll make *you* crawl to me. Would you like that?"

She whirled around, biting her lip hard. An overbright emerald gaze collided with his, the outrage that she was aiming for failing spectacularly. No, that was *intrigue* simmering like banked flames in those expressive eyes before flicking to what must be a very avid audience behind them. "Stop it," she said, breath hitching when his brow arched. "You're being crude."

"Never took you for a coward, Poison *Ivy*," he teased.

She huffed a breath and glared. "And you're a rake!"

"Haven't you heard? Rakes can be an excellent resource for anyone looking to explore their inner seductress."

Her mouth opened and closed, the scattering of freckles standing out like stardust beneath that fiery blush. "I will *never* need...oh, sometimes you are unspeakable!"

"Only sometimes?"

Briar bared her teeth in a feral smile. "Lushing, I swear to the heavens above that I will cut you dead and end this preposterous engagement, and all our efforts will be for naught, if you don't cease whatever this new game of yours is immediately. We are so close. Don't lose focus now because you're bored and need a distraction or simply want to be a pest." She smiled up at him, playing it up for their audience, though her gaze was pure smelted steel. "Soon, you shall have the right girl on her knees...as you desired. But mark my words, that will *not* be me."

Christ, the challenge was fucking irresistible.

But Jasper chuckled and relented. He'd respect her wishes...for now. Because if the last few weeks with her had shown him anything, it was that Lady Penelope could never, *ever* compare to the seething tempest who stood in front of him without an ounce of compliance in her body.

Not yet, anyway.

No, Penelope wasn't the one he wanted at all. He wanted a magnificent, ambitious siren with a tongue that didn't hesitate to slice a man to ribbons, an incisive, imaginative brain that would put a prodigy to shame, and a heart so big it took his breath away.

And now, he had the perfect strategy to woo her.

One she would never see coming.

CHAPTER EIGHT

Briar paced her study, staring at the words she'd just written and crossed out, and rewritten again. Ink splotches were speckled everywhere, and she'd almost thrown the bloody inkpot and her uncooperative quill into the wall.

Her contrary muse had returned and then vanished again, which was beyond frustrating, especially after Theo had asked her to publish the next volume sooner, given the demand. He'd promised they would print a thousand copies, nearly double the amount of the last printing.

If she didn't get her scattered thoughts together, there would be no Lady Ivy! However, something else—no, *someone* else—kept taking up the entirety of her brain. That deuced earl. The constant innuendo was maddening, turning her efficient writerly brain to depraved mush.

Ever since the ball, something had evolved anew between them, and it wasn't just his unseemly insinuations of things he had no business knowing. It was as though he could see who she really was, hidden behind all her thick layers of defense. But how could he? No one knew that, least of all her. But for the first time in her life, Briar wanted what Lady Ivy did.

With *him*.

Which would be a disaster. If their kiss had proven anything, it was that opening Pandora's metaphorical box would be a mistake. This was why she needed someone like the viscount. He inspired nothing. No lust, no interest, no curiosity or care.

She had goals. And plans. She had to stay focused on the prize...which was Preston, *not* the earl.

"My lady," a footman interrupted. "You have a caller."

Ah, perfect timing. Vesper had said she was going to stop by. Briar needed to get some of these confusing qualms off her chest, and who better to confess her fears to than one of the trusted Hellfire Kitties, even if it was the bloody blight's own sister.

"In here, Ves," she called out, not bothering to tidy up the mess with parchment strewed everywhere. She didn't call for her lady's maid because she would not need a chaperone, nor did she bother to smooth her messy hair or wrinkled dress. Vesper wouldn't care.

However, it wasn't Vesper who entered...it was Viscount Sackley.

Stunned, Briar peered owlishly at him. "My lord, this is a surprise."

"Lady Briar," he greeted with a bow. "I trust you are well."

"I am. I wasn't expecting company. Well, not you, I mean. Please, sit." She glanced at the desk, gut clenching at the handful of Lady Ivy chapters written out, though it wasn't likely that he would know what they were. The man was used to reading sermons, not sensation fiction.

He smiled and took the nearest armchair. It was strange how she'd thought him handsome before. Now his hair was too colorless, his eyes were the wrong shade of blue, and his mouth was thin instead of full. Briar shook her head. She wasn't interested in him for his looks, only his name. Oddly thankful that the door remained open, she peered at him. Perhaps she should send for her lady's maid.

"You've ink all over your dress," he chided. "Did you bathe in it?"

Briar blinked at the jab. Swallowing any retort and reminding herself what was at stake, she smiled politely and perched on a seat. There were footmen right outside the room—she'd hear him out and then he would leave. "What brings you here today, my lord?"

A pale gaze studied hers. "I have come to reinstate our engagement."

Briar blinked at the abrupt pronouncement as he stared at her expectantly. Did he expect her to swoon with gratitude? She should have felt happy that she'd gotten what she wanted, but Briar felt nothing, not even satisfaction. "What about Lady Penelope?"

"What about her?" the viscount asked.

Indignation sparked. Penelope might lack all the personality in the world, but she was still a human being who had feelings. Why were men like this? *Not all men*, her inner voice instantly chimed. "She is your fiancée."

"She is of no consequence," he said dismissively. "I acted in haste that morning when I saw you participating in such vile propaganda. However, I am a forgiving man. As my wife, you will naturally curtail all activity with Viscount Amberley's wife and those women."

Briar frowned. "Were you following me?"

Something off-putting gleamed in his pale stare. "A lady should never keep secrets from her husband."

"You're not my husband," she said. His fingers squeezed on the armrests, and she had the distinct impression that if she'd been near enough, they would have closed over any part of her.

"Not yet," he replied. "But let us move past this, shall we? I'm willing to let your transgressions be forgiven. You have need of me, Lady Briar, and I have need of you." He leaned forward. "In fact, you require guidance and deliverance."

The way he said it had her stomach churning for no reason. His voice was even, his face calm, but something in that fervent stare rode her instincts hard. She suddenly did not feel safe at all. "Are you forgetting *I'm* engaged?"

He sneered. "To that scapegrace? Come now, Lady Briar, you know you only did that to save face with the *ton*. He is wrong for you. He is a degenerate who is lost, and I refuse to let him besmirch you."

A shiver slid over her spine when he reached for her knee, and she jumped up, out of reach. "I'm not one of your flock, Preston," she said, and his eyes flickered at the informal address, but suddenly, Briar didn't give a shit about displeasing him.

He stood slowly, and she reversed a step. He matched it, and she did the same until the back of her thighs hit the desk. The viscount's hand lifted, and she flinched, but he only moved one of her curls to the side before running his knuckles over her cheek. His *bare* knuckles. When had he removed his gloves? Her stomach roiled.

"I've missed you," he murmured. "This brazen defiance. Flaunting yourself in that harlot's dress as if I wouldn't notice. Flirting with that libertine, meeting with those women in seedy taverns, breaking bread with filth and lowering yourself to such debasement." A tip of his finger trailed down her neck to her shoulder and then down the back of her arm. "You think I did not see you? You think I cannot see the sin hovering around you right now?" His gaze fell to the desk behind her, even as her breaths tightened to panicked bursts. She wanted to move, to *shove* him away, but she was frozen in place like a terrified statue. His fingers stopped above her elbow. "You test me sorely, little dove."

Time went still. *Little. Dove.*

"It was you," she said, breathing out. "You sent the notes. You *were* following me."

"As I said, you require guidance. You've strayed, and it was my duty as your future husband to keep my eye on you." His gaze dropped to the desk again. "Nothing you do is hidden from me. That *man* on Holywell Street," he murmured. "The purveyor of foul iniquity will be imprisoned."

Oh, God. *Theo.* "What have you done?"

"My duty." His nostrils flared. "I miscalculated with Lady Penelope, thinking you would see the error of your ways and beg for my forgiveness. But perhaps a firm hand is what you need." He pinched hard, the tender skin at the back of her arm smarting. That would leave a bruise. Tears welled of their own volition, and she cursed her own weakness.

"Get your bloody hands off me," she whispered, body shaking like a leaf.

"Such insolence," he said as he struck like a snake, his other hand gripping her chin with a force that felt like it would crush her jaw.

"Fuck you!"

His eyes narrowed to slits. "I will enjoy breaking you of such vulgar habits and bringing you to heel."

Desperate, Briar scrabbled behind her, grasping for anything solid on the desk until her fingers closed around a letter-opener. Without a second thought, she pressed the sharp point into the soft flesh of his torso where only the thin fabric of his shirt kept it from his skin. "Get. Off. Me."

"How dare you strike a peer?" he snarled.

She pushed harder, jaw gritted. "You dared strike a peeress first."

"And who would believe you, little dove?" he crooned. "You're a woman. It is my word against yours."

"My very degenerate earl would."

Briar saw the moment the viscount lost control, the rage snapping in his eyes her only warning. She'd frozen earlier— she wouldn't now—but if she physically harmed the viscount, she would be charged by the police. However, she had a voice...and it was meant to be used. Before he could shift his palm to silence her completely, Briar opened her mouth and screamed as loudly as she could.

The viscount dropped his arms and backed away in an instant as the nearest footmen rushed in. "My lady, is all well?"

She stalled them with one hand and nodded, composing herself before glaring at the viscount. "Don't ever come near me again," she said to him in a low, furious whisper, still grasping her weapon.

"I have already informed your father, Lady Briar," he said in a saccharine tone for the benefit of the hovering servants. "It will be done."

"And I will *never* marry you." She turned to the stone-faced footmen. "See the Viscount Sackley out, please. And summon my *brother*, Inspector Givens of the Metropolitan Police, at once. I wish to report a crime."

She might only be a woman, but she was one with very useful connections.

The viscount's gaze glittered, lip pulling into a sneer as he stalked from the room.

Briar closed her eyes, her body slumping weakly while the concerned maids clustered around her. "I'm fine, I promise. Let me know when my brother arrives."

Sometime much later, nearing the evening hours, Briar found herself in front of the Earl of Lushing's residence at St. James Square. She had no idea if he was home, only that she'd slipped away for a walk to clear her head following her fraught conversation with a murderous Levi, who'd been a hairsbreadth from getting the rest of their brothers and going after Sackley.

After nearly an hour of walking aimlessly, her feet had led her here.

To *him*.

Briar swallowed and lifted her hand to knock, only to let it fall back to her side.

God, what was she *doing*? She might have changed her mind about Preston, but Lushing still had a chance with Penelope, and now that the girl was free, he could. Besides, the earl probably wasn't even at home. He was a busy man, and he spent most of his hours at Lethe. In fact, she should have gone there first if she truly wanted to see him.

"Briar?"

She turned, and there he was, sliding from his horse and looking so deliciously windblown and perfect and *real* that her chest ached. Her lip wobbled. When his brows dipped in concern and he came toward her, she burst into tears and threw herself at him.

Without hesitation, he caught her, arms banding her tightly to him. "What has happened? Are you well?"

"I am now," she sniffled and then groaned with her head in his chest, mortified at her horridly public display. "Can we go inside, please?"

"Are you alone?" he asked, and she knew he was only asking for her sake. He was an unmarried gentleman, after all, and she was at his private residence. Girls had been ruined for less, not that Briar gave a whit about propriety right then.

Shaking her head, she inhaled the intoxicating cedar-and-spice scent of him, deciding that she could stay quite happily right where she was as long as he'd let her. "I think that ship has sailed, Lord Lushing. And considering we are engaged, the tongues will wag regardless."

"*Still* engaged?" he asked. "I heard that Sackley broke it off with Lady Penelope. I assumed he would come directly to you."

"He did. I turned him down." Her voice shook, and she

pressed her cheek harder into his chest, eyes stinging anew at lingering echoes of the viscount's touch.

"You did?"

"He's a monster." A small sob tore through her. "Please, Jasper, can we go inside? I only need a moment, and then I promise I will leave."

He released her slowly, waiting until she was steady before rapping on the door. After a handful of seconds, his butler let them inside, and she kept her head low until the earl dismissed his man and they stood alone in the foyer. Gaslights flickered over them.

"Briar," he said gently. "Look at me."

She didn't want to. She knew exactly what he would see. Levi's reaction had been awful; she suspected that Lushing's would be worse. But she also couldn't hide forever. Slowly, she lifted her head and knew the exact moment he took in the bruises on her chin when an *inhuman* growl ripped from his chest.

"Who. The fuck. Did this. To you?" His entire body locked up with rage, tremors rocking through him, the sheer savagery on his face the expression of nightmares. "Was it *him*? Did he fucking put his hands on you?"

Briar nodded. "Yes, but—"

"I'll fucking kill him!" He whirled to leave, but she grabbed his wrist. He stalled at her touch, his big body shaking with whatever monster he was trying to keep at bay. "I need to go. He has to—"

"No, stay. *Please*."

Hunching over, he quaked from the force of the fury barreling through him, fists balling at his sides. "I know...but I can't...I want to...*fuck*. Briar, he *touched* you. He *hurt* you."

"And I'm here now," she said, closing her much smaller hands over his white-knuckled fists. "Safe, always safe. With you. Levi is taking care of him, I promise. Just be here with me, please."

The earl stared down at her, those endlessly deep blue eyes swirling with so many emotions that she could barely pick them apart. Fear, wrath, concern, infinite tenderness. His gaze darkened as it flicked to her chin. "Does it hurt?" he whispered.

"No." She slid her hands up his arms and looped them around his neck. "But I keep thinking about it. I need to erase his touch. I need to forget how his eyes looked at me. How his voice sounded. I don't want to think about him anymore." She paused with a shudder. "Make me forget, please."

"What are you asking, Briar?" he rasped.

Her eyelashes fluttered as she dug for courage...for the strength to ask for what she wanted. What she *needed*. "Put me on my knees," she whispered. "I want to kneel for you."

Her words detonated into the silence between them. And then he groaned, a sound of pure unadulterated need. "*Fuck*, Sweetbriar." He stared wildly down at her. "Are you certain? If we do this, I might not be able to let you go. I don't know if I *could*."

"Then keep me," she said simply.

Their gazes collided and ignited. Heart crashing into her ribcage, Briar waited. She'd made her desire clear. It was up to him to accept the overture because, as much as she wanted him, consent went both ways.

If he said no, out of any sense of misguided propriety or skewed sense of duty, she would fucking *die.* Right now, she needed him more than she needed air.

But then she gasped as he swooped her up into his arms and raced them up the stairs to his bedchamber before kicking the door shut. "Last chance. Are you certain this is what you want?" he asked, chest heaving. "Yes or no."

"*Yes.* Make me yours, Jasper."

For a handful of seconds, it was pure chaos as they tore at each other, their mouths colliding, fusing, softening, biting, and sucking while their hands furiously worked at buttons and fastenings. Outer trappings went first, and then her dress pooled next, followed by her corset, chemise, and stockings. Impatient fingers ripped his own fine linen shirt down the middle, and his boots careened across the room, until at last, they were both panting and nude.

Briar stared, mouth drying, her entire body quivering with need. He was the most gorgeous thing she had ever seen. She always knew he was fit from boxing, but he was hewn like a warrior. Everywhere she looked, her awe grew. That broad chest, dusted in bronze-red hair, was a mesmerizing landscape of masculine strength and beauty. His limbs were all long, honed muscles and sculpted sinew—rounded shoulders tapering into corded forearms and thick thighs flowing into strong calves. Those stacked ridges of his abdomen flexed, making her eyes drop to the sleek muscles pointing right to his very erect cock. She gulped.

Well, that was going to take work to fit.

His laughter filled the room, and she realized she'd murmured that out loud. "Don't worry, Sweetbriar. By the time I'm finished with you, I'll have you so drenched you'll be more than ready for me."

Her cheeks flamed at his lewd words.

"Take the pins out of your hair," he said. The soft command made her tremble, but she did as he asked, feeling the curly mass tumble down.

"I knew you would be this beautiful," he whispered reverently, a hand rising to sift through the loose curls and then drifting down to cup her breast. He traced the curve with his thumb. "Fucking perfect."

She wanted to say she wasn't, but a stroke just below her nipple made her whimper instead. Briar didn't love her breasts—one was slightly larger than the other—and she always wished they were smaller, so the difference wasn't so noticeable. As much as she wrote to empower women to love their bodies, she was insecure about her own. When he cupped them, she wanted to push his hands away, but his touch was too distracting.

Her taut nipples tightened more as he flicked gently over them with each thumb and then ducked his head to take one peak into his mouth. She forgot all about her imperfections. Heat sluiced through her as he sucked, the light swirl of his tongue sending a desperate ache to her core. He licked and sucked and nibbled until she was writhing before moving his attention to the other breast. By then, her core was throbbing indecently, every pull of his absurdly talented mouth echoing between her legs.

"I'm ready now," she whined.

He chuckled against her skin and then bit her nipple hard enough to make her squeak. "You'll know when you're ready."

"When?" Her voice was so needy and breathy, it was unrecognizable to her own ears.

"When my tongue is buried between your legs and you're soaking me and begging me to let you come." God, his *words*. The thought of his mouth there made heat explode in her veins.

Jasper found her lips again, kissing her hard until she was seeing stars. Then he released her and walked backwards until his calves touched an armchair. He lowered himself into it. Dazed, Briar watched him, her limbs shivering. His eyes were hot on her, staring ardently at the breasts he'd left damp and aching, and then descending to the dark curls at the apex of her thighs.

She wanted desperately to cover herself, but kept her hands at her sides. She was so wet, she could feel the moisture clinging to her inner thighs. Could he see? Alarm filled her, but when he licked his lips with a groan, staring at her with so much hunger, she felt powerful.

Embody Lady Ivy. Let him look.

Briar wasn't submissive by nature, but she craved this. She wanted her brain to shut down for once, and she trusted that Jasper could give her what she needed. It was cathartic to hand herself over to someone so completely...to relinquish control. To *yield*.

"Eyes on me, Briar."

A shudder shook her limbs. Obediently, she did as he asked. The earl stroked his length, drawing a whimper from her when his thumb slid over the top, smearing the drop of fluid there. Her mouth watered with the urge to taste it herself. A moan flew from her lips, her eyelids fluttering.

"Do you want this?" he asked.

"Yes."

"If there's something I say or do that you don't like, just

say stop, and I will." He met her gaze, making her bite her lip at the pure lust she saw burning there. "Nothing will happen that you do not desire. Do you understand? I need your words, Briar."

"I understand. I'm to say stop if I'm not comfortable."

"Good girl," he murmured, and her eyes practically rolled back into her head at the praise. "Oh, you like that, do you?" he crooned, watching her when she nodded, every inch of her on fire. His mouth curled into that wicked smirk she loved.

"On your knees," he commanded. Briar dropped like a stone, breath turning jerky, and her vision darkening at the edges. "Hands on the ground."

She complied, the second graveled, "good girl" nearly making her lungs give out. Her blood thundered between her ears, all her senses fraying by the second. She felt indecently exposed without a stitch of clothing, but it wasn't enough for her to want to stop. Her fingernails dug into the thick pile of the rug to ground herself into the moment.

"Now I want that arse in the air, and I want you to crawl *slowly* to me when I tell you to."

Bloody hell. It was indecent the way her core clenched at the darkly sensuous growl in his tone. Her nipples were so tight she could feel her heartbeat pulsing in them, but she curved her spine, pushing her hips high. A pained sound ripped from him, and she could see the darkness in him roiling to the surface, barely leashed. It exhilarated her seeing him so affected.

"Good so far?" he rumbled.

She nodded.

"Words, Briar."

"Yes. Good." Her voice was a hoarse rasp. Gracious, if she could barely form words now, what would happen by the time she reached him?

"Then crawl."

It took every ounce of her concentration to even breathe with all the sensations rocketing through her at that hushed gravelly order. But she put one hand forward and then the other, following with each knee.

God, the action was so degrading, and yet when she looked at him, all she saw was need. Lips parted, eyes *burning*, his hand worked his weeping cock. He looked at her like she was the only thing he ever wanted.

Like he wanted to devour her alive.

Like she was *everything*.

CHAPTER NINE

Jasper was going to fucking die.

The sight of Briar on her knees, that stunning, curvaceous body glistening like oiled bronze beneath a delicious sheen of sweat, had him so damned hard he could barely think. Her body undulated like some kind of sinuous jungle cat as she closed the distance to him, the look of pure trust on her face and the dark sensuality of the act she was performing a volcanic combination. He'd never seen anything so fucking beautiful in all his life.

When she was a few feet away from him, he lifted a hand. "Stop."

"Why?" she asked, worry creasing her brow as she halted.

"Did I give you permission to question me?" he said sharply. A burst of pique flashed in that green gaze, but she bit her lip and shook her head. "Now sit up and spread your legs. Then touch yourself and tell me how wet you are."

She blinked. "Oh."

"*Now*, Briar."

Her pupils dilated at the dark snap of his tone. Pushing back onto her haunches, she put her hand on her mound and then hesitated. He lifted a brow, and her cheeks went red.

"You can stop this at any time. Just say the word."

"I don't want to stop," she whispered.

Ever so slowly, she slid her knees apart and her fingers slid south. He could barely see anything, but this wasn't about him; it was all for *her*. Her jaw slackened as two fingers dipped into her cleft. The soft gasp that left her told him what she'd found.

Jasper's cock throbbed violently with the need to be buried right where she was.

Soon...

"Are you wet for me, Sweetbriar?" he asked.

"Yes."

His voice emerged like pure gravel. "Show me."

Obediently, she lifted two fingers that glistened wetly with her arousal. *Fuck.* He bit back a groan at her dripping fingers.

"Good girl," he said, her entire body quivering with pleasure at the praise. "Now put them in your mouth and tell me how you taste."

Briar went still, her eyes boring into his. "You want me to taste myself."

"Yes."

His body felt hot and on edge as they stared at each other. She seemed curious, not repelled, but everyone had their limits. Was this when she would finally ask him to stop? Jasper knew they were crossing lines that few gently bred ladies would have any inkling of, and making her crawl to him like this and then lick her own arousal were intense, especially for a novice.

But his daring virago didn't resign. No, she held his gaze as she lifted her fingers slowly, that small pink tongue darting out to lick the moisture off the tip of her index finger. He didn't even have to tell her to suck as she sank both digits into her mouth and moaned. She fucking *moaned*.

"Words, Briar." Fuck, he could barely find coherence himself.

"Sweet." She slid her tongue between her fingers, making him suck in a breath as he imagined that mouth around his cock.

His staff throbbed in his hand, and he cursed softly, the entire game forgotten. "How are you this fucking perfect?"

With a pleased smile, she grinned at him like a devious siren, that emerald gaze flashing with mischief when she went back into position on all fours.

Dazed, Jasper watched as she crawled the rest of the way to him and placed her hands on his knees. The shy innocence from her face earlier was gone. In its place was a woman who had shed her inhibitions and now had something new in her sights.

Him.

"My turn?" she purred, pushing his knees wide and wedging her way between them.

The switch in disposition had Jasper reeling. Hell, how had the tables turned so thoroughly? She was no longer the submissive, shy kitten who had crawled across the room to him. No, this was *Lady Ivy*, in the flesh. She peered up at him through a fringe of dark lashes, taking the corner of her lower lip between her teeth.

"Words, Jasper."

He wanted to chuckle at her playful tone as she stole his earlier words, and if he wasn't so choked up by his feral arousal, he would. As it was, even her breath feathering over his groin had him thinking about anything else but the feel of those lips gliding over the length of him. His cock bobbed, and he squeezed ruthlessly, throttling back the orgasm that had been building at the base of his spine from the moment she'd said, *put me on my knees.*

"Yes," he ground out. "Touch me."

"You're wet, too," she said, swiping a finger through the mess of fluid on his crown. He'd been stone-hard and leaking like a faucet since he kicked the door shut. He nodded, hissing at the sensitivity as she scooped the moisture up and brought it to her lips. Her eyelids fluttered as she savored him on her tongue.

Fuck me.

Savoring him, Briar licked her lips, and it took every ounce of his concentration not to grip hold of that gorgeous wealth of hair and drag that lush mouth onto him, but this was her show. She tugged at his fingers, releasing his grip on his shaft, and made a contented noise in her throat when the whole of him was visible to her greedy gaze. She traced the vein along the underside with a fingertip, making him hiss again when she crested the top.

"Does that hurt?" she asked.

"No. It feels good. Too good."

"Do you want more?"

"Yes," he groaned when she leaned over to blow a stream of air on him.

Jasper was at her mercy. She would set the pace and lead

where she wanted. If she wanted to torture him, he would endure. If she took it further, he would be grateful. If she wanted to stop, he would. He might die, but he would obey.

He'd do *anything* for her.

Luminous green eyes met his as she inched closer between his legs. "May I?"

"*Please.*" The word was an unhinged sound.

His eyes rolled back in his head when she closed her hot mouth over him, swirling her slick tongue around the tip, her small hand replacing where his had been. Her fingers didn't touch, and her grip barely covered half of him, but when she worked his shaft counterpoint to the deep suction of her mouth, he saw fucking stars as he hit the back of her throat.

"Fuck, love, like that. *Yes.*"

Her mouth felt like liquid velvet, the soft press of her tongue driving him wilder with each seductive pass. Jasper was already beyond aroused, and her enthusiasm made up for her lack of experience. But after only a minute or two, he pulled her gently off him. He wasn't going to last.

"I'm not finished," she protested, wiping her lips.

He winked. "I know, but in my book, ladies come first."

In a glorious display of well-muscled flesh, the earl reached underneath her arms and rose, taking her with him as if she weighed nothing. Briar knew he was strong, but she couldn't help an appreciative sigh from escaping.

Wrapping her legs around his waist for purchase, she clung to him as he walked them both toward the bed. With each step he took, she bit back her whimpers when her sensitive nipples abraded against his coarse chest hair and her drenched core slid against his grooved abdomen.

She was obscenely wet after pleasuring him.

Licking her swollen lips, Briar savored the decadent, earthy taste of him that lingered on her tongue. She leaned into the gratification she'd felt when she'd taken Jasper into her mouth and the noises he'd made, even the hedonistic enjoyment she'd felt tasting her own arousal.

Ever since she'd first written a scene involving pleasuring a man by mouth, she had wanted to try it. Briar had no idea if she'd demonstrated much skill, but from Jasper's shudders and moans, he had to have liked it. He'd almost been too thick to fit in her mouth, and she could barely take much of his length inside without gagging, but she'd enjoyed every second of it. Her cheeks were hot from how brazen she'd been, but well, Lady Ivy wouldn't have any shame.

You're not Lady Ivy.

No, she wasn't, but Lady Ivy had become the understated symbol of a sexual revolution, especially as it pertained to *this* and the fact that women were also deserving of pleasure. The ideas of morality that sexual intercourse was sinful or dirty were archaic notions. Having—and enjoying—an orgasm had no impact on a woman's modesty or her ability to be a good wife and mother. If anything, it made women happier and healthier.

As Minthe had succinctly said, the divine creator wouldn't have included a button if they didn't want someone to press it. *Repeatedly.*

Briar couldn't help her grin at the courtesan's irreverent words. But Minthe wasn't wrong. People weren't born with shame—it was a learned and taught self-conscious behavior.

Shame had no place when it came to loving every part of oneself.

"I can feel how wet you are," Jasper said when they reached the bed, his hands sliding down to the curves of her bottom. She froze. Clearly, from her splayed position, she'd smeared her arousal all over him.

"I'm sorry," she murmured automatically, and then realized she wasn't sorry at all. Men didn't apologize for being hard—it was a natural response. "Wait, I'm *not.*"

He grinned. "You shouldn't be, I'm desperate to get my mouth on you so that I don't waste another drop." And that was all the warning she got before he tossed her to the mattress and dove between her legs like he was starving and hadn't had a meal in weeks. "Fuck, you're stunning here, too. I knew you would be. All pink, claret, and dewy, like a blossoming rose."

"I..." Words failed her as he smirked, staring up at her like a devoted sybarite from between her thighs.

God, it was indecent seeing herself open like this...with him right *there,* her most private place on display. She instinctively tried to close her knees, but he held them open.

"Stop whatever it is you're thinking right now, Briar. And don't you dare hide from me."

"I'm not. I wasn't."

"What did I say about lying?" Still holding her gaze, he inhaled deeply, and she wanted to squirm with embarrassment. "Now, listen," he growled. "It's my turn, and I'm going to lick this sweet cunt until you're begging me to stop. I'm going to make you come all over my mouth at least twice, and then I'm going to make you come again on my cock. And you're going to take every inch of me like a good fucking girl."

Her eyes bulged. Oh, *fuck*. The *things* he said would make a seasoned courtesan blush. The sounds of those deliciously filthy sentiments falling from his aristocratic mouth did dreadful things to her constitution! Bloody hell, her cheeks were on fire.

"Jasper..."

He slapped her smartly across the lower lips of her sex, and she squealed as a blaze of heat spread across her mons. "Eyes on me," he rumbled roughly like a savage creature guarding his prize. "Not another sound. Leave me to my feast, or I won't let you come."

Feast? Was he— Oh, God, he *was*...

Nothing short of a miracle could have stopped the obscene moan from leaving her lips when her wicked earl put his mouth to her and licked her from entrance to clitoris with the flat of his tongue. The sensation was glorious. He did it again, as if she were a cream ice melting in the sun, swirling the bundle of nerves at her apex as her body dissolved into quivers of pure need. Briar had touched herself before...but *this* was sublime in a way that she'd never experienced, and when he sucked, her spine felt as though it might snap.

Pleasure ratcheted as his tongue lashed against her, and she whimpered when she felt a finger circling her entrance. He slid in easily, the slickness paving the way for him to add another on the next pass. Her tight passage squeezed around him, the sensation of fullness making her groan when he split his fingers apart within her, stretching her gently.

"What are you doing?" she gasped.

"You need to be able to take me," he said, lifting his head.

She peered down at him, blushing at his glistening ruby-red lips before her eyes went wide as she took his meaning. "You're much bigger than two fingers."

His mouth quirked, those ocean-blue eyes sparkling. "Yes. I've got you, Sweetbriar. Trust me, love."

With a hungry sound, he set his mouth to her again, his fingers working in clever harmony with his tongue, and she felt the pressure when a third finger pressed inside. It pinched slightly, but it wasn't long before she stretched to accommodate him. His other hand was not idle, reaching up to twist her nipple as she writhed.

Sensation streaked through her, like stars shooting through her veins, intensifying until her entire body shook. The knot in her core tightened and tightened, the tension unbearable, and then she broke with a shrill scream...the paroxysm taking her in its grip, waves of bliss crashing through her.

The grunts he made were just as loud as he drew out every drop of pleasure from her trembling body, his mouth gentling slightly, but not relenting as she came back to herself. Her hand wound into his hair when he moved his fingers, still lodged deep inside. "It's too much, please. I can't..."

"One more, Sweetbriar," he coaxed. "God, look at you. You were made for this. Made for *me*."

That ravenous gaze roamed over her flushed sex as if his hunger might never ever be sated. As if he could gorge on her forever. He started out slow, his mouth pressing kisses to her inner thighs, so gentle that she barely felt his touch. Then he started lapping with soft nudges. Briar stared at the mural above his bed, colors bursting behind her eyes. How anyone could lie there and think of England was beyond absurd, come to think of it.

She could barely think of her own name...

Briar suppressed a giggle, but then a hot lick of pleasure twined through her when he did something with his index and middle fingers, curling them toward him and brushing a spot inside her that made her vision wobble.

"Oh, what is that?" she whispered. "Again."

She felt him smile against her skin, and when he acquiesced and brushed the spot on her front wall, slow and sweet, she didn't make a single sound. Her body fluttered. She let herself sink into the blissful sensations as he strummed her pliant body to perfection. In a suspended state of rapture, she rode the waves of spiraling euphoria until they flung her into the cosmos to float among the stars once more.

Afterward, he kissed his way up her sated, boneless body and held her in his arms.

"Now you're ready," he whispered. Jasper took her mouth in a drugging kiss as he settled his hips into the cradle of hers, his erection prodding her swollen center. "How are you feeling? We can stop now, if you want."

"What about you?"

He smiled. "This isn't about me, it's about you."

God, this man. Always thinking about her comfort. She stroked his face and then kissed his mouth gently. "No, it's about *us*," she said. "I want you. Wholly. Completely."

His beautiful eyes stared down into hers, relief and desire mingling there. He swallowed hard, his throat working. "I need to tell you something. I have a...confession."

He looked so serious, so *uncertain*, that she wanted to erase the small groove from between his brows. She reached up to brush the hair from his temple with a puckish grin. "What? That you've fallen in love with me and can't bear to be parted from me another day?"

"Yes."

She blinked, all playfulness evaporating, when that single word sank in. "I...beg your pardon?"

His lip quirked. "I love you, Briar. I wanted to tell you before we became lost in the heat of the moment. I think I've been in love with you since the day we met."

Briar felt those whispered, hesitant words burrow into her soul as a tear slid out of the corner of one eye. She could have written a thousand Lady Ivy stories, and she never would have been able to convey the wealth of feeling that ignited in her chest right at that moment. Her body felt too small to contain it all...this profound emotion expanding like the sun was bursting from her.

"I love you, too, Jasper."

He kissed her nose, but not before she saw the glossy sheen in those bottomless blue eyes. "Just remember who said it first."

She huffed a laugh. "You simply cannot help yourself, can you?" Heart impossibly full, Briar rolled her eyes and wrapped her legs around his waist. "Now make me yours so you can tell me what a good girl I've been for you."

Chuckling, he kissed her slowly, worshipping her mouth, and then dipping to each of her breasts, until she was writhing anew beneath him. He knew exactly how to touch her to coax and tease each ounce of pleasure from her body, and within minutes, every inch of her was vibrating. He notched himself to her entrance, and Briar took a deep breath as he began to push inside. Even with all his earlier preparation and how soaked she was, he was big.

"So fucking tight," he groaned. Withdrawing, he shuttled back in, repeating the motion and each time easing in a little more. Briar whined, grinding up against him even as he kept a measured pace, so he didn't hurt her. The sense of pressure and fullness was almost too much, but she wanted more.

She stared up into those limpid blues. "Harder. I won't break."

A muscle hammered in his jaw as he held himself up, muscles straining. He pulled out and drove back in. *Hard.* Despite the bite of pain, she sighed at the stretch, feeling her walls flutter around him. One more thrust, and when he was finally fully seated, they both shuddered at the perfect, sublime fit.

"Mine," he rumbled.

Her blood was on fire as need throbbed deep in her core. "Now, Jasper. Give me everything."

Jasper hitched her leg over his hip and withdrew before slamming back in. He groaned. Fuck, the silken clasp of her body was everything. He watched her with every thrust, seeing what made her whimper and what made her scream, because by the time he was done with her, he wanted her to be a sobbing, incoherent mess.

He kissed her mouth, her breasts, any skin he could reach. Every nerve inside of him sang—the pleasure simmering in his veins heated to a dizzying intensity with each steady thrust. He slid his hand between them, stroking the swollen bud that made her tight passage clench hungrily around him, and drove her desire higher.

"More," she begged, clutching at him, her nails digging into his shoulders. "Faster. Please, I need…"

He didn't need convincing. "I know what you need."

Jasper withdrew completely from the snug sheath of her body, scooting backward to take her clitoris in his mouth and suck hard, moaning at the lush taste of her, before he flipped her body over and situated her on her hands and knees. "You looked so pretty like this, crawling to me, that all I could think about was fucking you."

His fingers collared her throat as he positioned his cock and drove back into her. Briar's spine arched, a scream tearing from her when he went much deeper than before.

"Oh, yes," she moaned. "*There.*"

Jasper grunted, the sensation of her choking his cock almost sending him over the edge. But he had more to do before he let himself finish. With a hand between her breasts, he pulled her up, still impaled on him so that her back was flush to his chest. He squeezed her throat, thrusting shallowly, and pinched her nipples, exactly as she had described in the scene he'd read.

There was one other part to the chapter that he'd practically memorized when Lady Ivy's lover dominated her in a way she liked. Slowly, he pushed her down, moving with her, his cock never leaving the heated grasp of her body, until her head hit the mattress. The position was degrading, but he knew she loved it. She'd written about it in explicit detail, after all.

He groaned low in his throat when she submitted so

beautifully. Jasper gathered her wrists behind her back so that she was helpless even as he pounded into her, pinning her into place and fucking her with ruthless determination.

"You feel so good, mistress," he crooned. Would she recognize the scene? Would she know that the words he used...were hers? "Such a good mistress taking every thick inch of your lover's wicked prick."

She gasped aloud. Jasper felt it the moment she realized what he was quoting when her body tried to strangle his cock.

"You are doing so well," he continued with a grin. Thanks to her own words, he knew exactly how she envisioned being taken and how she adored being praised. "Who owns this greedy, sopping little quim?"

To his delight, she complied, her words thick with lust.

"You do," she whimpered. "I'm yours. I'll always be yours. I want you. I ache, please, I want it all—"

After that, there was no finesse as he fucked her, only raw desire, heat, and ravenous *need*. He unleashed, drilling his hips into her body until the only sounds in the room were the slaps of skin, punctuated by feverish moans. The friction was exquisite. The storm began to build at the base of his spine, the orgasm that he had been holding off for what felt like hours flying along his veins. Jasper curled his hand around to pinch her clitoris.

Briar screamed, back bowing, her body spasming around him.

"Fuck, fuck, *fuck*," he chanted.

He felt his own desire rising like a geyser on the heels of hers. With one last thrust, Jasper withdrew and emptied his seed onto the sheets with a guttural roar, his cock pulsing with a violent orgasm that made his vision grow hazy. Pleasure blasted through his limbs like lightning, and he flew apart into a million pieces.

Eventually, they collapsed onto their sides, breathing hard as their bodies quivered and convulsed for what felt like an eternity. He kissed her temple and tucked her into him, pulling her smaller, sweaty body into the curve of his. He was almost half asleep when she stirred.

"How did you...?" Briar trailed off as if she couldn't quite ask the question. "Did you read...?"

Jasper chuckled and buried his face in her soft curls. "You're a very talented writer, Sweetbriar. In fact, I believe that I might be your most ardent admirer."

CHAPTER TEN

"Hullo! Briar, are you even listening?" an exasperated voice said. "Good heavens, it's like talking to a rock."

Briar blinked as a scone waved wildly in her face. She jolted, flushing slightly when she realized that Vesper, Laila, Effie, and Nève were all staring at her with raised brows as if they'd been talking to her for some time. She'd nodded at the right moments, sipped her tea, and eaten her sandwiches during their usual afternoon tea party, but her brain had wandered.

How could she reply to her best friends that no, she *hadn't* been listening because all she could think about besides the fact that the Earl of Lushing was an incredibly generous lover, that he had told her he *loved* her, or the fact that he had read Lady Ivy...and now he knew her deepest, darkest secret. *And* claimed he was her most devoted admirer.

So much so that he'd *acted out an entire scene* from her last book, one she hadn't even recognized until she was in the throes of an orgasm so powerful, she'd been lost to utter oblivion for a handful of minutes. It had only been in the aftermath, lying in his arms, when the pieces—and *her* written words—had truly connected in her head. How long had he known? She trusted that Lushing wouldn't expose her.

The viscount, however, was another matter. She had much worse to worry about. Sackley had sent a final note to Lethe with an ultimatum: marry him or he'd expose her to the *ton*.

Honestly, it was a miracle that her emotional state wasn't worse. Between her feelings for Lushing and the unforgettable evening they had shared, as well as Sackley's threats of being exposed to the *ton* as Lady Ivy, she was pulled thin.

Briar pushed a wan smile to her lips. "Sorry, Ves. I have a lot on my mind right now."

Her friend wrinkled her nose. "Your head has been in the clouds since you arrived for tea. Has something happened?"

"I don't want to dampen anyone's spirits," she replied.

Laila patted her arm. "That's what we are here for, Briar. The good *and* the bad. Now, spill what's on your mind before I'm forced to take desperate measures like convincing the girls to tickle you for information."

Briar couldn't even force a smile. She met their curious and concerned gazes. "Viscount Sackley knows about Lady Ivy. He says that he's going to have Theo, my publisher, arrested, and he's holding the information over *my* head as well." She hesitated when they instantly expressed noises of alarm. "Apparently, he has been keeping track of my where-abouts for months. He knows about Lady Amberley and the suffragist meetings, as well as what I do"—she hesitated for a moment before drawing in a deep breath—"at Lethe."

"What *do* you do at Lethe?" Nève asked curiously at the same time that Effie let out a jubilant noise of victory.

"I knew it!" Effie crowed when everyone stared at her. "I told Gage when we were in Scotland that you were much too familiar with that club after his boxing match. You knew those corridors like someone who had been there often. He told me to respect your secrets and that when the time came, you would share them. Is that time now?"

"Yes, I'm sorry I didn't tell you," Briar said weakly. She bit her lip and glanced at Vesper before swallowing. "I approached Lushing a while ago about hiring women who had found themselves in compromising situations like Minthe. He was the only one I knew in our set who was in a position to give anyone a second chance and employment, so I made him a proposition. I might have forced him to comply, in hindsight."

Vesper snorted, interjecting, "Forced him, my twitching eyeball. Of *course* he agreed because my brother has carried a bloody torch for you since the dawn of time. Haven't you realized by now that he'll do anything for you?"

"Not if the idea doesn't have merit," Briar said flushing, knowing this was the moment when everyone would expect her to say something scathing about the earl, but she couldn't bring herself to do so. She reached for her teacup and took a gulp of her lukewarm tea. "He agreed to help in part. I said I would pay them out of my own income, which fortunately I had from my pin money and the profits from Lady Ivy."

"Wait, does Lushing know?" Nève asked, shoving a large bite of seedcake into her mouth. "About her?"

"He does." Briar willed her rising blush away, but it seemed that she could hide nothing these days. Especially when it came to the earl. Her cheeks flooded and her friends —the queens of theatrics—pounced.

"What? Since when?" Laila shrieked.

Effie's eyes rounded. "Why the blush? My God, has he *read* Lady Ivy?"

"How did he find out?" Vesper demanded.

Briar chose the easiest question to answer first, ignoring Effie's because no explanation could properly suffice—*yes and he made me come so hard by seducing me with a reenactment of my own salacious imagination that I was rendered temporarily insensible.*

"I don't know when, and I suspect he could have overheard one of us at some point." Briar waved an arm at their messy tea table. "We are not exactly the quietest bunch. Also, I might have also let slip that I enjoy uplifting women with my stories during an argument, so he put two and two together. The man is ridiculously observant."

She didn't add the information about his other nickname, *Poison Ivy*, which wasn't such a stretch from her nom de plume. That had probably been silly of her, but maybe somewhere deep down, Briar had intuitively *wanted* to use one of his silly pet names.

"Yes, he's very vigilant," Vesper said with a sly look. "Especially when he's obsessed about something."

"Or *someone*," Effie added, attempting to peer into her soul again.

Briar swallowed her snort. She wanted to scream that

she *knew*...and that she was just as smitten. But she and Lushing hadn't discussed making their true feelings public, despite their ongoing fake engagement. That revelation would have to wait.

"So, what happened with Sackley?" Nève asked, frowning. "Did he threaten you? You said he was holding the knowledge over your head as well. What has he done?"

"He came to the house and said he wanted to reinstate the engagement."

"Tell me you didn't take that louse back," Vesper said. "I saw him criticizing poor Penelope last week about slouching, and she looked quite petrified."

Wincing, Briar shook her head. "No, I did not. Because, well, there's more." She paused to collect herself. "I never told you any of this because I thought I could manage him. I was so focused on *my* goal that I didn't see...what I should have."

This was the part she didn't want to talk about, but Briar also didn't want to hide what the viscount had done, and clearly what he was doing to Penelope as well. This was how men held power over women...out of fear and not being held accountable for their words or actions.

Reaching for courage, Briar rubbed at her arms and then reached for one of the linen napkins on the table. She dipped an edge into a pitcher of water and then rubbed it gently over the Crème Céleste facial paste she had applied on her chin to conceal the unsightly purple bruises in the shape of large fingerprints.

Tears sprung to her eyes at the collective sounds of outrage when she set the napkin back down.

"He *dared*!" Laila snarled.

Effie and Nève wore matching expressions of pure fury—they had both been the targets of cruel men in the past. "Oh, Briar, I'm so sorry," Effie seethed, her pale face mottled red with rage. "I hate him!"

Nève was visibly shaking. "How many times has he done this?"

"Never on my face," Briar said. Peeling down her glove, she turned sideways where bluish-purple shadows marred her skin there, too. "Usually here. He likes to pinch whenever he's displeased."

"I'm going to fucking eviscerate that sackless bastard," Vesper growled. "We will murder him, and no one will ever know where to find the body. Who was that woman you told us about, Briar? The one with the arsenic?"

"Madeleine Smith," she said, recalling when she'd jokingly told Effie that they could make the Duke of Vale disappear when she'd found out about the asinine wager he'd made to court her in London. All had ended well, thankfully, with no murders. Or time in prison for any of the Hellfire Kitties. "You would have to get in line. Levi is furious. Lushing, too."

"My brother will rip him limb from limb," Vesper bit out.

"Levi says there is no proof to bring any charges against him, and before you get up in arms about the bruises, it would be my word against his in a court of law. No one has ever *seen* him doing anything who can corroborate my claims." She let out a hollow laugh. "It's ironic, isn't it? I *help* women escape men like him, and here I am, caught in the same trap. And I didn't even realize it."

"He needs to pay," Effie hissed.

Briar nodded with a resigned shrug. "Trust me, I had a

hard enough time convincing Levi and Lushing not to do anything that could send either of them to Newgate. And Sackley is much too cunning to allow himself to be caught. For now, I simply must be careful...and make sure I'm not alone."

"So, he can just hurt you and get away with it?" Vesper said through gritted teeth.

Briar understood her rage. She loathed the feeling of being so powerless...especially in the eyes of the law. "You all know what we're up against, what I've been fighting for years with Millicent and Katherine. We don't have a voice or the vote, or anything to protect ourselves from men like him." A choked sob caught in her throat, and her friends immediately crowded around her. "I thought once we were married, his attention would be elsewhere, but he's more fixated than I ever imagined. He wants to *rehabilitate* me."

"What?" Laila whispered.

"As though I'm something ruined or broken in need of repair."

Nève scoffed. "You're not!"

"None of us are. And we're all wonderfully imperfect and flawed in some way," Effie added. "I love animals more than people, well, except you four, and Gage, I suppose. And I love dildos. In fact, I own a dozen of them in various shades of colored glass. They have names."

Everyone stilled and then started snorting.

"My brain doesn't work like everyone else's. I love swearing," Vesper chimed in. "And I have a decidedly indecent penchant for swiving my husband in public places. Especially on giant stone dinosaurs."

A slew of giggles ensued.

"I was paid for coitus," Nève volunteered. "I'm the richest courtesan duchess in all of England. And France!"

They giggled harder.

"I like being spanked," Laila admitted, and then went crimson.

They roared, collapsing to the grass in a heap of skirts and crinolines. Briar wiped at her eyes as they all flopped to their backs like the demure ladies they were. The housekeeper and a handful of maids bustled over to clear the table, their faces amused.

They were more than used to the Hellfire Kitties, who never did anything they were supposed to. Who were unapologetically unconventional. Who were spurned and envied in equal measure by high society. Who fought for justice and lived by their own moral codes. And three of them had married dukes, one a marquess, and well, Briar supposed that she might someday marry an earl.

With laughter in her heart, she stared up at a very blue sky, several shades lighter than the blue she loved. *Ocean-blue with flecks of cobalt at the center. Eyes that a girl could willingly drown in.*

"I gave Lushing my virginity," she said.

Dead silence ensued before screaming rent the air, and she was suffocated by four ridiculous women who piled on top of her in an undignified heap.

"WHAT?" The biggest screech was unidentifiable.

"I am finally getting my own sister!" That muffled shout was from Vesper, obviously.

"How was he at the blanket hornpipe? Did you ride the rantipole?" Effie teased, throwing Briar's own words back at her when she and Vale had been courting, and someone made a gagging noise.

"Vile, I do *not* want to hear about my brother like that."

Effie giggled. "And yet you read about it with no qualms? In all her volumes, Lady Ivy has seduced nine redheads, three brunettes, and two blonds. Do the mathematics; red hair is simply not that common."

"Ten, if you count the real thing," Briar added with a grin.

"*Ahhh!*" Vesper shrieked. "*He* was your inspiration in Lady Ivy? Bloody fucking hell, I'm going to be ill. Move! Or I shall cast up my accounts all over the lot of you!"

Briar smashed a palm over her own mouth to block her giggles at Vesper's histrionics.

By God, she loved her friends.

When the chaos had calmed once more and the others had gotten in all the bawdy jabs they could about Lushing's red hair, prowess, and stamina, they lay in silence, still piled on each other. Someone's leg was jammed over her hip. Her head was currently in Vesper's lap with her feet trapped beneath Laila, who was half stretched over an entangled Nève and Effie.

"Is the engagement still on then?" Nève asked.

"It was never real to begin with," Briar replied softly. "Lushing has never actually asked me to marry him."

"He and I will have words," Vesper promised.

With fond exasperation, Briar glanced up at her friend. "Promise me you won't. If we are meant to be, we will be. Right now, I have bigger things to worry about...like whether that sackless viscunt will expose me to the ton. I don't care about my reputation, but I don't want to hurt my parents and expose them to scandal."

"Cool your heels! Did you just say vis-*cunt*?" Vesper asked and then cackled. "Viscunt Sackless shall rue the day he touched one of us! I might not be allowed to commit murder, but when I'm done with him, no one will dare welcome him anywhere, I vow it."

Nève nodded. "We might not have lawful power, but we have *influence.*"

"We are like chai," Laila added. "You never know how strong we are until you drop us in hot water."

Effie reached for Briar's hand and squeezed. "Weak men will always be intimidated by formidable women, and when they try to break us, they learn that we're not so fragile. We fight back and we don't suffer fools gladly."

Sitting in his coach, Jasper stared at the red velvet-lined box containing the elegant gold ring that had belonged to his mother. He intended it to be an engagement gift for Briar. While the clarity of the square-cut emerald could never hope to match the brilliance of her eyes, it was a close enough substitute that his heart sped up just looking at it. A halo of rose-cut diamonds surrounded the glittering, faceted stone. It was the perfect ring...for the perfect woman.

His stomach clenched with nerves.

She could still say no...

Especially since his second gift for Briar was the purchase of a property in Bath that he intended to give her, regardless of whether she accepted his offer of marriage or not.

He'd just made two stops. One to visit his father, the allegedly ailing and bedridden Duke of Harwick, whom Jasper had caught playing a boisterous round of cards with his valet and his coachman. The duke had miraculously taken a turn for the better, only just recently, according to his private physicians.

Jasper had had his doubts, but he didn't blame the crafty old man for forcing his hand. After he'd asked for his late mother's ring, the duke had brightened and clapped him vigorously on the back, forgetting that he was supposed to be infirm.

"Who is the lucky girl?" his father had asked. "Lady Penelope, is it? Vesper has kept me abreast of gossip in the *ton* when she visits, though your sister is adamant that the young lady isn't the one."

"Vesper is usually right," Jasper admitted with a resigned laugh. "No, Father. I intend to wed Lady Briar Fairview."

The duke's eyes had sparkled with a shrewd knowing. "The lively chit who writes letters to Parliament on women's suffrage? If I recall, she and Dr. Garrett worked with John Stuart Mill for the petition to the House of Commons two years ago, garnering some fifteen hundred signatures in support of their right to vote." When Jasper nodded, his father had grinned. "She's the one who has always twisted you up in knots and never tolerated any of your tomfooleries. I like her very, very much."

"That's the one," Jasper had replied drily. "Glad you approve. Now I'll leave you to your clandestine card game. Don't wager away my inheritance, will you?"

Jasper's next stop had been to Briar's father, the Earl of Rubens. At first, the earl had listened politely, saying that the viscount had already renewed his suit, but after Jasper had given him a short summary of Viscount Sackley's foul behavior and treatment of Briar, he'd swiftly changed his mind. Jasper had also made arrangements to purchase the unentailed property in Bath outright when Rubens had explained that his title would go back to the crown upon his death. If it was part of her dowry, that meant it would belong to her husband.

Jasper intended to keep it in a trust for her for as long as she lived. Even if she married, it would remain hers. He was an avid supporter of the Married Women's Property Bill in Parliament that had recently been submitted to grant married women the same property rights as unmarried women, to allow them some financial independence. There was no guarantee it would be approved, however. And he knew how much her childhood home meant to her.

When the coach finally arrived at Lethe, Jasper knew something was wrong the moment he walked through the doors. Hapless servants were running around while others were openly weeping. Had there been an accident? Had someone died?

He turned to the grim-faced factotum. "What has happened?"

"Minthe is missing," he said.

Jasper frowned. "What do you mean, *missing*? Did she not come in this afternoon?"

"Yes, according to the servants, she was here. And then a message came for a delivery for her or Lady Briar specifically."

Jasper's hackles raised, cold dread sluicing through him. "*Or* Lady Briar?"

"She was not here, but Minthe went down to retrieve it." The factotum scowled. "And then she disappeared. One of the scullery maids said she saw her getting into a fancy-looking carriage. The maid remembered it clearly because they were joking about Minthe finally having a gentleman suitor who was making an honest woman out of her."

"Any sign of who it was?" Jasper asked, though he had an inkling. The factotum shook his head. "Have one of the grooms saddle my horse."

"Yes, my lord."

If he recalled, the viscount had a property just outside of London. He raced upstairs to his office and sorted through Minthe's meticulous, alphabetically arranged ledgers. Sackley had applied for membership less than a year ago, and though it had not been granted—membership at Lethe was *exclusive*, after all—his brilliant bookkeeper had kept a detailed record of every applicant, including their many addresses, vices, debts, and incomes.

"There you are, you bloody bastard," he muttered, memorizing the location before opening a case and retrieving a pistol. He made sure that it was loaded before buckling a harness with a holster that went under his coat.

His office door slammed open, and a tempest whirled inside in the form of one curly-haired, green-eyed woman.

"Jasper! Olsen just delivered a note while I was at tea with the girls that Minthe is in trouble." Briar's eyes went wide as they dropped to the weapon. "What on earth is that for? Where are *you* going?"

"I suspected he was the one who snatched her," Jasper

said. "The description was the same as the person who delivered the notes for you." He gnashed his teeth. "The prick was hoping for you, but he got Minthe. Let me guess—your note said to exchange yourself for her?"

Briar nodded and showed him the note, which matched the address in the ledger. "Yes, and it's his estate. The one just outside of London, near Papa's ancestral seat in Surrey."

"I gathered," he said, drawing her close and kissing her soundly. "I'll be back soon. Stay here. Do *not* leave this building."

"I beg your pardon?" she growled. "Don't you dare order me about. I am going with or without you. Minthe is *my* friend. And Sackley is—"

"Is what? A dangerous man?" Jasper glared, his temper sparking. Did she not realize what a deadly situation she could be walking into?

"I'm armed," she said viciously. "And I am an excellent shot. Don't do this, Jasper. Don't dismiss me because I'm a woman."

"I'm not," he gritted out, scrubbing a hand through his hair. "I cannot abide by the thought of you getting hurt. Not when he's already hurt you. *Fuck.* Don't you understand?" His voice broke on the last...the image of that fucking monster putting his hands on her, making him see red. His chest was so tight he could barely take in a single sip of air.

"So, my feelings about *you* getting hurt matter less?" she asked quietly. "Is that it?"

"Briar, *please.*"

She walked up to him and cupped his face. "I love you, Jasper, but you do not own me or my choices. We can go together, or I will go by myself. Those are the options available to you."

They stared at each other in a silent, fraught standoff, and all he could think was how goddamned beautiful she was, like an avenging angel full of might and righteous fury about to rain hell upon her enemies. The truth was, even if he were her husband, he would never take away her choices, even though the thought of her in harm's way made the beast inside of him go rabid. Already, after what Sackley had done to her, Jasper wasn't sure if he could restrain himself and not flatten the man.

"You're armed?" he asked eventually. She nodded, showing him the weapons at her waist, and he also saw that she wore her Seven Dials men's attire beneath her cloak. At least that was much less noticeable than a gown. "You'll stay behind me and do as I say." He saw her face and the mutinous line of her mouth. "*Please*, just give me this, Sweetbriar." He was begging, and he knew it, but he needed to feel like he was in control of *something*.

"Very well," she said. "I will do as you say, *if* it makes sense."

If that was all he could get out of her, he'd take it. Jasper bent and kissed her urgently, claiming her mouth with all the desperation and fear inside of him. She kissed him back just as fiercely.

They descended the stairs together, but when they got outside Jasper let out a curse. A carriage full of women stood in front of his residence. He blinked. All of Briar's friends, including his sister, were crammed into the coach in various states of disarray.

"No," he said. "Whatever this is, it's *not* happening."

"We are here for Minthe," Vesper said firmly, her face defiant as if expecting him to make a fuss, which he was absolutely on the verge of doing. "We must stop that monster once and for all."

Dear God, they were going to be the death of him. Jasper calmed himself and tried to stay clearheaded. The wrong words could have a mutiny on his hands, and they really did not have time to argue. If he could get Briar to stay with them, even better. Perhaps, if he were lucky, this would all work out naturally.

"I'm riding my horse," he said, climbing into the saddle of his waiting stallion. "It will be quicker than taking the roads. But someone needs to inform Inspector Givens of the viscount's threats as well as the fact that he has kidnapped an innocent woman. You ladies can help with that."

Vesper nodded. "Very well. Be careful, Brother."

Briar grabbed the bridle before he could leave. "Jasper Lyndhurst, if you even *think* of leaving me behind, I will never forgive you, and you can kiss this engagement and *me*, goodbye!"

"There's only one horse," he said weakly, and for the life of him, he couldn't understand why all the women in his immediate vicinity, with the exception of the stone-faced warrior queen holding his mount in place, dissolved into raucous laughter.

"Only one *anything* has never stopped a determined man," someone trilled.

"Or woman," another added.

With a stoic look, Jasper hoisted Briar up to sit in front of him. Her pert arse, unhampered by any skirts or crinolines, ground down over his thighs, and he suppressed a groan when she wiggled to get comfortable. This was neither the time nor the place to sport an inconvenient erection, but when had his body ever behaved when it came to Briar Fairview?

Never...the answer was never.

CHAPTER ELEVEN

Briar's heart was pounding in her chest as she and Jasper rode over the rise, cutting through her father's property and approaching from the west. They made the sixteen-mile trip quickly, but when every minute counted, quick wasn't fast enough. But she was hopeful that Preston would not hurt Minthe, not when he clearly knew that Briar would come in exchange. But the man was unhinged, and that meant he was unpredictable. Minthe was in trouble because of her.

They dismounted, tying the horse to a low branch before cutting through the woods. For a big man, the earl moved quietly, and the only sounds were their footsteps crunching on the forest floor and the bubbling sounds of a small brook.

"This way," she said in a low voice. "This spring will take us to the northeast side of his property, where the kitchens are."

Jasper still looked uncomfortable, his face wreathed in grim lines, but he would have to get used to her taking the lead. Briar had spent many winters growing up on this estate, so she knew the area like the back of her hand. She liked a protective man as much as anyone, but there was a huge difference between being protective and smothering someone. She knew he was afraid *for* her, however, and that mollified her somewhat.

They moved more slowly when the turrets of the main house came into view. The viscount's house was quiet—most peers were settled in London proper for the season, but that didn't mean no one was there. It also didn't mean this wasn't some kind of elaborate snare, designed to get what he wanted. The note Briar had received ordered her to come, or he would hurt Minthe and expose Briar's secret.

If Sackley intended to force her to marry him, would he have a vicar there with a special license? He'd almost been a vicar himself, but that didn't mean he could perform the nuptials. Then again, he didn't need a priest to force her hand. An unscrupulous man only had to get an unwed woman in a compromising situation, and they would be forced to wed.

Many a fortune hunter had done such a thing to a lady to marry her and gain control of her fortune. It was despicable in the extreme...yet another way that men could control women. That was what would happen to the property in Bath—as part of her dowry, it would become her husband's. When he'd initially spoken to her father, Preston had agreed not to sell it, but she didn't trust a single word out of that man's mouth.

The sound of a carriage pierced the air, and Jasper hurriedly pulled her out of sight, though they were still deep enough in the woods not to be noticed. Frowning, they both watched as a fancy coach drove past the gaps in the trees and turned toward the main house. Another conveyance followed right after. Did the viscount have company?

Something didn't feel right.

"We should wait," Jasper whispered. "The sun is going down, and we will have the cover of darkness to work out what's happening. That will also give your brother some time to get here with reinforcements." He caught her worried expression. "Sackley won't do anything to Minthe until you arrive. He was at Lethe for you, not her. She's bait. Did the messenger ask you to read it in front of him?"

"Yes. And I had to send back a reply that I understood."

"Good," Jasper said. "The messenger will be paid to return with your reply, and we will have a small window. Not much, but enough for us to not be so exposed. For now, we wait."

He lowered his big body down with his back pressed to the trunk of a large oak, and after a moment, she did the same right next to him against the tree. They sat in silence, but Briar was too agitated to sit quietly. She peered up at him. "Do you think Minthe will be all right?"

"Minthe spent a decade in the demimonde. She knows how to handle herself."

Briar's chest ached, her stomach churning with worry. "You didn't see him. He was so angry."

"We will get her back," Jasper said, squeezing her hand and pulling her into his arms.

Briar let some of her rattled nerves be calmed by his warm strength. She was furious at the viscount, but she was frightened, too. At Lethe, she'd seen evidence with her own eyes of men's cruelty to women. And Sackley was a monster.

He'd kept that affable mask in place so long and so well, but it had finally dropped that day in her study.

She'd seen his *true* face.

If anything happened to Minthe, she'd never forgive herself.

Curled against the earl, she watched as the shadows of the trees grew longer, the evening gloom creeping over the wood as the sun descended. It didn't take long, but after a while, Jasper shifted and sent her a silent nod.

They stood and crept down the tree line, keeping to the shadows before racing to the nearest wall of the house. Inching their way around to where she knew the morning salon was, Briar peeked into the window and swallowed a gasp.

"What?" Jasper whispered.

"Penelope is there, and her mother."

"Why would she—?" he began, but then clamped his mouth shut as he was likely realizing what Briar already knew.

If Sackley was planning to compromise her, he needed a witness with an unimpeachable reputation from the aristocracy. A countess would be more than enough. But how would Sackley have convinced a woman he'd jilted to help him? Even an oblivious Penelope wouldn't be *that* magnanimous.

Briar peered in the window again and frowned. "There are other faces I recognize, too. This doesn't make sense. Why would—?"

The sounds of a scuffle made her whirl. She was much too late to react as she watched Jasper go down from a blow to his head, but when she reached for her pistol and opened her mouth to cry bloody murder, a cloth beneath a huge hand covered the lower half of her face. A sweet smell invaded her nostrils.

What was...that...*oh*...

It was her only thought before her eyes rolled back in her head and darkness took her.

The sound of three gunshots made Briar lurch up.

Her eyelids cracked open to blurry faces as light speared into them. She groaned, shutting them and squinting. Her head felt like it was splitting open, and her stomach churned with nausea. Dimly, she took in that she was on a sofa. She was also wearing a light pink gown and dainty white gloves. Briar didn't remember getting dressed for a party, though this wasn't one of the dresses she owned. She never wore taffeta. Or such a dreadful jejune color.

She wrinkled her nose and winced at the ache in her skull. The gunshots came again, and she realized dully that someone was clapping in front of her nose.

"WhereamI?" The words emerged in a jumbled mess as if her tongue was dry and too thick for her mouth.

"Welcome back, dove," a male voice said.

"Preston?" she mumbled when he came into view, and then she reared back. "You took Minthe." And then she grimaced as the events of the last few hours flew back to her disoriented brain. "You drugged me! Where is the Earl of Lushing? You'll go to prison if you've done anything to him, I swear it."

"Don't worry about him. Worry about me."

Briar wheezed and tried to sit up, but a sudden wave of

dizziness made her waver. "Where the hell is Minthe? If you've hurt her, you gutless prick, I'll kill you myself."

The viscount tutted, his lips flattening with displeasure. "The first thing we will need to do is deal with that vulgar tongue of yours." He sniffed. "But for now, we have guests, and you must be seen. Be sure to be convincing of our reconciliation, or your friend will pay the price."

"Where. Is. She?" Briar reached for her belt with her weapons, but all she got for her troubles were handfuls of ugly taffeta. Her belly roiled with something bitter. Had *Sackley* dressed her? She tugged at the ruffles. "Did you—? How am I in this?"

The viscount pinched his lips. "Your virtue was quite protected, little dove. Don't worry." He pointed at a terrified-looking mouse of a lady's maid whom Briar hadn't noticed cowering in the corner. "Nora did an excellent job preparing you for our very special occasion." He lifted her pocket pistol. "And if you're looking for this, well, such a weapon is not fit for a lady, is it?"

She clenched her jaw. "I'm not doing a single thing until I see that Minthe is unharmed."

Anger sparked in his pale irises as he signaled to Nora, who scurried from the room. A few minutes later, she returned, followed by the man who had hit Jasper with a truncheon. He looked like a hired thug, but Briar was more focused on the woman he held roughly.

Minthe's hair was tangled, her cheek bruised, and her clothing ripped as if she'd been in a fight for her life, but her eyes were simmering with rage. *Good.* Anger was strengthening; despair and defeat were not.

"Minthe, did they hurt you?" Briar asked.

"I hurt them worse," her friend said.

The thug scowled, and Briar noticed the oozing scratches down each side of his face and what looked like bite marks on his forearm.

"Go and see if the earl is alive, and if he is, take care of it," the viscount barked, making Briar jolt. She'd fallen uncon-scious before she saw what had happened to Jasper, but a blow to the head could be fatal. Horror and panic twined in her belly, but neither emotion would help her now. Jasper was strong; he'd make it.

Right now, she had to save Minthe and herself.

After the man left, Preston prowled behind her friend with her gun in his hand. He leaned in and sniffed her hair in a way that made Briar's flesh crawl. How had she missed all the signs that he was a zealous predator? Bloody hell, had he sniffed *her* when she hadn't been aware? Studied her every move with those reptilian, unblinking eyes?

Briar stifled her shiver. She wanted to signal something to Minthe to give her hope—that Levi was on the way—but the viscount wasn't stupid. He was careful and slippery…a fact only obvious now in the glare of hindsight. Perhaps Briar could find a way to get help from any of the people who were in the drawing room. She needed time to come up with a plan. Or perhaps she could do something now so Minthe could escape…

"What now?" she demanded rudely.

That priggish gaze lifted. "Well, Lady Briar, since you asked, if you're obedient and behave, this lucky little harlot will live." The viscount lifted her pistol and dragged the muzzle down Minthe's discolored cheek to her throat to the visible embroidered edge of her corset. Her friend quaked, though she tried to hide it. "If you defy me, she won't."

"What is it you want, Preston?" Briar asked.

His face twisted. "We will marry this evening. I have obtained a special license. If you do your duty with the decorum I expect, she will be released." He lowered his voice to a hiss. "And for extra incentive, if you say a word about any of this, your secret alter ego won't be a secret anymore. Think about your parents. The friends you will harm by mere association. Your pristine reputation."

"I don't care about reputation," she shot back.

"No?" he said silkily. "Do you think the men in Parliament would think so highly of a woman of your questionable character, *Lady Ivy*?" Briar ignored Minthe's soft gasp. "What would happen to your petitions and signatures? Your influence? Your precious vote?"

Bloody hell. He was bluffing. If he exposed her, he would be tarnished as well. But could she risk it? Could she risk all the work she had done? Briar lifted her chin. "I am already engaged."

"Not for long. I *will* have you," the viscount said, a fanatic light in his eyes. "You, little dove, were put in my path for a reason. You are mine."

"I'll never be yours."

"I will enjoy clipping those wings. You *will* repent, you *will* cease all depravity, and you *will* be the most perfect, most virtuous wife."

Oh, if he only knew. Briar burst into laughter, snickering so hard she nearly toppled over. When he glowered at her, she laughed harder and clutched at her stomach. He took a menacing step toward her, gun lifted. Briar wasn't afraid. He wouldn't shoot her, not if he needed her, and for all his posturing, he had guests. Murdering his bride would ruin his plans.

Besides, she wanted to make sure he moved away from Minthe.

"Stop this at once," he spat.

Briar wiped her eyes. "Oh, Preston, you silly fool, why would you want someone who has already given her virtue to another?"

He froze, that feverish gaze slamming into hers. "You *lie*."

"It's true. My very virile, debauched earl fucked me until I couldn't walk. Made me scream his name to the heavens until I was hoarse." She pretended to swoon and gave a melodramatic moan that would have made Lady Ivy proud. "Made me come so many times, I soaked the bedsheets."

Minthe was staring at her with her jaw on the floor. At any other time, Briar would preen in the blatant approval she saw there, right before dying of embarrassment. But now, all she was thinking about was survival and keeping Preston's attention so Minthe could run.

"Go," she mouthed to her, and then angled her body so that the viscount's view was partially blocked.

"Harlot!" the viscount snarled.

"That word doesn't have the power you think it does," Briar scoffed. "They're women who know what they want and how to get it. And most of all, they're very good at picking out those who know how to last, if you know what I mean."

A demented sound ripped from the depths of him. His face twisted, and he *lunged* at her. Briar tried to jump out of the way, but her limbs were still weak from whatever anesthesia he'd doused her with, and she stumbled. His fingers caught on a few tendrils of hair at her nape, and she winced as they came loose in his hand. Briar gasped. Her *coiffure*!

It was still in the clever updo she'd fashioned earlier— the tiny lady's maid still crouched in the corner hadn't touched it, so that meant Briar *wasn't* weaponless. The viscount charged for her again, and she dodged his attack clumsily, while wrestling with the special pin holding her wealth of hair in its coil. She didn't want to accidentally impale herself. It was a cleverly redesigned two-pronged hatpin made from Damascus steel with sharpened ends— the perfect hidden weapon.

"You're going to be very sorry when I get my hands on you, little dove."

When he lunged for her again, she was ready, aiming for the most lethal spot—the neck. Briar struck. But the viscount shifted at the last minute, and the hatpin sank into his arm. He howled, his face going puce with anger.

Damn and blast. She had wounded him *and* managed to enrage him.

With a growl, he rushed her, and in her haste to escape him, her foot got caught on the base of the divan. His fingers snapped out and banded around her neck, yanking her back. Briar crashed into his body, and she nearly vomited when her bottom encountered his groin. He was *hard*. Dear God, he was enjoying this. His hand tightened around her neck, and she gasped for air as he deprived her of it.

"Pres—" Her fingers scrabbled at his unbreakable grip. "S...stop..."

Suddenly, there was a loud crash, and his grip loosened as he slumped to the ground. Wheezing, Briar hauled huge gulps of oxygen into her lungs and spun to see Minthe standing over him with the remnants of a large vase in her hand. "I told you to run!"

"You wouldn't have," Minthe shot back with a shaky grin. "Thank me later. And don't think for a second we aren't having a conversation about a certain writer."

The sound of a gun cocking made them both freeze. Sackley stood. "Neither of you are going anywhere. Now *sit down* or I shoot."

Blood dripped into Jasper's eyes.

Trussed up with his arms behind his back, his head throbbed, and his shoulders burned, but he'd been able to pick at the knots with his thumb. He'd almost worked them loose when he heard noises outside the potting shed or wherever he was.

Fuck.

He picked at the ropes faster, but it was to no avail. Footsteps halted outside, then there was a murmur of low voices. He closed his eyes and evened his breathing. He might have a chance if his assailants thought he was still unconscious. The door pushed open.

"It's the earl, Inspector," someone said softly, and Jasper's eyes flashed open. Levi Givens, Briar's brother, came into view, his frame outlined by the sparse moonlight. Relief swamped Jasper when his bonds were cut by the man who had spoken.

"Lushing," Givens said as Jasper stood, blinking woozily

and swiping at the congealing blood on his brow. "Where's my sister?"

"Sackley has her," he said hoarsely. "How many men—"

But his words were cut short when someone—clearly not one of Givens's—approached. Givens and his man took him down in relative silence, but Jasper was already hurtling toward the house. He had to get to Briar. He hoped he wasn't too late, and he didn't know what he was running into, but he didn't care.

Christ, how long had he been out?

Enough time for the bastard to compromise her?

There was no time for subterfuge. People in the *ton* knew who he was, and he would use them as eyewitnesses, just as Sackley had intended to. Jasper entered the front door, past the gaping butler, past the foyer of well-heeled people.

"It's the Earl of Lushing," someone whispered.

Another let out a shriek. "He's bleeding!"

"Has he been in a brawl? Look at him."

He knew how he appeared. Jasper didn't care what any of them thought. He searched through the rooms, not seeing Briar or the viscount, and ventured deeper into the house. His gaze snagged on a footman. "Where's your fucking master?"

"U...upstairs, my lord. The master suite, east wing."

Not wasting a second, Jasper took the stairs two at a time on soundless feet, ears pricked just as a crashing sound of a dish breaking came from the far end of the corridor. He veered toward it and picked up his pace until he reached a pair of closed doors.

"Now sit down or I shoot," a man snarled.

It was *him*. A seething Jasper pressed his ear to the wood.

He forced his boiling blood to calm because he had to be smart. If Sackley had a gun, it could go off.

"Preston, please...I'll do what you want, just let her go."

Briar!

"Shut up. I need to think. Look at the state of you. You can't go down there looking like that. Girl, go fetch a comb and some powders, and send a servant for some water. Now!"

Jasper stepped back just as the door opened and a thin, terrified maid hurried out. He put a finger to his lips as her eyes rounded when she caught sight of him. Most servants wouldn't be privy to their master's plans, especially one who looked this frightened. Jasper jerked his head for her to leave.

He had seconds, if that, before the door latched, which would lose him precious time. Kicking the door open, Jasper briefly caught sight of Briar and Minthe on a seat—*both alive*—before springing for the man to his left. Sackley held a pistol, but Jasper had faced many an armed robber at Lethe. Without hesitation, he dove low, going for the knees. Both men tumbled in a heap, thudding to the carpet.

Dimly, he heard Briar scream his name over the sound of the blood rushing between his ears, but his fists were moving, crashing into any part of the viscount as they rolled. The gun was caught between them as they grappled for it. Jasper absorbed a punch to his torso and then grunted when Sackley's skull crashed into his already wounded temple. Fresh blood spurted, temporarily blinding him.

Get the gun, get the gun.

He almost had it, but suddenly, a loud crack made his ears ring as more wetness drenched his face, a stinging pain searing through his breastbone. Jasper's head banged backward hard as he crashed down. A second gunshot reverberated, but he couldn't make sense of it. Blinded by blood dripping into his eyes, he could not hear or breathe. Everything felt heavy. The viscount stared viciously down at him, his weight crushing Jasper's throbbing ribs, those pale eyes open and locked in rage.

Christ, his fucking chest was burning...

"Jasper!" Briar cried. Hands tore at him until he was lying on his back, gasping for breath. She tugged at his clothing, searching for any wounds. "Have you been shot?"

There were people in the room—he caught sight of Givens—but he only had eyes for one. His Sweetbriar. God, she was beautiful. Her hair fell around her face in a silken cloud as she crouched over him, those green eyes glossy with tears and glittering brighter than the emerald in his pocket. He cupped her face with a bloodied hand. "I love you so much."

"Jasper, did he get you?"

"No," he rasped. "Just the burn from the muzzle. I'll live."

They both stared at the viscount's unmoving corpse beside them as Briar burst into sobs and peppered his face with kisses. "God, I thought you were dead. You silly, beautiful fool. He was armed. How could you be so reckless? I could have lost you."

"You'll never lose me. You would miss me too much. You're stuck with me like an in-growing toenail, remember?"

She sniffled, smiling through her tears, her eyes flickering as she remembered their banter years ago in their back garden when she'd first met Nève. "How do you remember these things? I didn't mean that."

"Yes, Prickles, you did. But I know a way you can make it up to me."

"And what's that?"

He fumbled for his trouser pocket, pulling out the small box and opening it. Her eyes widened. "I think you should marry me, love. My odds of survival chasing after you in dangerous places are dwindling by the day. A man needs assurances."

She giggled. "Does he?"

"The sooner I can call you my wife, the better. Now be a good girl and say yes."

Her eyes dilated, but she gave him a teary nod. "Yes, Jasper. Always, yes."

EPILOGUE

When everything was said and done, and the dust had finally settled, the official report was that Viscount Sackley had been dispatched by the Metropolitan Police for attempting to murder a peer. The scandal surrounding his obsession and kidnapping of two women had made the rounds in the gossip rags with much speculation as to the viscount's proclivities. It was curious that the people invested in shaming others usually had the most dreadful secrets.

As Vesper had discovered, Penelope, as it turned out, was an enthusiast of Lady Ivy. Apparently, the viscount had come upon the volumes she had collected and threatened to expose her so-called perversions, unless she did what he asked. Much to Penelope's delighted shock, a large package featuring signed copies of Lady Ivy's adventures had been recently delivered to her home.

So, Briar's secret alter-ego was safe.

She knew that Minthe would never say anything, though the woman had interrogated her like a seasoned investigator in the carriage on the way back to London. The girls, even

Effie, had been relieved that both she and Minthe had escaped mostly unscathed after the ordeal. Briar and her friends had wept and hugged, clutching each other like the unbreakable sisterhood they were.

Then Vesper had somehow gotten it in her head that Minthe and Levi seemed to be exchanging looks of desperate yearning, according to Vesper at least, and she'd had to be steered away immediately from resorting to her meddling, matchmaking ways. Briar had chuckled. If it were meant to be, it would be. Minthe was a few years older than her brother, but if they could make each other happy, then that was all that mattered.

After they had both been seen by Dr. Garrett and pronounced healthy and hale, things fell back into a quasi-normal routine.

Briar spent most mornings with the London National Society for Women's Suffrage, her afternoons at Lethe, and her evenings at balls and parties for the remainder of the season with the rest of the Hellfire Kitties, keeping her eye out for influential supporters as well as those who might welcome earnest new employees looking for a chance of a better life. In her spare time, she continued to write.

Well, she *tried*.

Despite Theo's shortened stint in prison for distributing illicit literature—Viscount Sackley's word was worthless—which Theo had assured her hadn't been the first time nor would it be the last, the demand for more of Lady Ivy's stories remained high. And not just from the ladies either. It seemed that her readership was growing, thanks to more open-minded Englishmen who wanted to keep their wives happy.

As long as she was willing to pen the books, Theo was happy to publish them and continue their very profitable arrangement. Though in truth, Briar wasn't sure what Jasper's feelings were on the whole thing, which was probably what was obstructing her muse.

The viscount's ugly words still lingered in her head.

As a lady who carried her husband's name, it was her marital duty to represent him well in society. She knew the earl *liked* her work, but it would never be considered a ladylike pursuit, nor an appropriate vocation for a future countess.

Perhaps the discussion would be better had sooner rather than later.

With that in mind, she knocked on his office door at Lethe. There was a scuffling sound before his deep voice said, "Come in."

"Am I disturbing you?" she asked, frowning slightly at his flushed face as he sat with one hip propped against his desk. Dressed in charcoal trousers, a blue waistcoat, and shirtsleeves with the cuffs rolled to display those thick veiny forearms that always made her insides fray, he looked wickedly handsome and entirely too pleased, like a cat who just devoured an enormous saucer of cream.

"Never. You were just the woman I hoped to see."

Strolling into the room, she glanced around, seeing nothing out of the ordinary, but he looked like he was up to something. With him, one could never be sure. She narrowed her eyes. "Why do you look like you're bursting at the seams? Jasper, what have you done now?"

He gave her a breathtaking smile; the *real* one she loved that made his eyes crinkle and those blue irises shimmer like the sea on a summer evening. "Because I have a surprise for you. Two surprises, actually. But first, you look like you've something on your mind. What is it?"

Oh, of course. *Lady Ivy.*

Briar inhaled a deep breath. "I need to talk to you about my writing," she said before she could lose her nerve.

Smile diminishing at her serious expression, he cocked his head. "What about it?"

"Since we are to be married, I was wondering if I should stop," she rushed out. "It's not the kind of thing that a lady should be writing about and—"

"Does it make you happy?" he asked.

She blinked. "Well, yes, I enjoy writing her stories. I discover more about myself every day, and I think she also brings joy, courage, and intimate agency to many other women. And men, too, I suppose."

"Then, keep doing it," he said with another of those heart-melting grins. "And I can wholeheartedly agree about the more joy part."

Her cheeks went hot at that—supposedly, he was obsessed with reading past iterations for *inspiration.* "But what if—"

Jasper dragged her toward him and pressed a finger to her lips. "But nothing, Sweetbriar. I want my countess to be happy doing whatever she loves. And it is my honor and privilege to support you in any calling you choose. I will give jobs to anyone you feel needs a second chance. If you continue to bring petitions to Parliament for women's suffrage, I will be your keen and faithful voice until you have your own." He winked. "And as far as Lady Ivy, well, we both know what she does to me."

"Jasper." She flung her arms around his neck and kissed him, drinking in his scent and the appreciative sounds he made. "How I love you!"

"Wait until you see these surprises; you will love me more." He grinned with a soft kiss to her forehead. "It's my goal to make you fall so deeply in love with me that I am imprinted upon your heart for all eternity."

"I suppose it's working," she said, heart squeezing at his playful sweetness.

Kissing her again as if he couldn't stop touching her, he turned to his desk to retrieve a document. It looked like something official, complete with stamps and signatures. Briar perused the length of it, catching sight of the address of her family home in Bath. "What is this? My dowry?"

"Not exactly. The property is in a trust with your name on it. I bought it from your father, and this way, until English marriage laws change, it will belong to you."

"Jasper, I—" Her jaw went slack as she stared at him. "You did this...for me?"

"It's yours," he said simply. "Just like everything I have will be yours, including this wonderful facility, even if English law does not explicitly say that. *Yet.*" He shrugged and wrapped his arms around her again, tucking her head under his chin. "This way, you know that your childhood home will always be yours."

This. Man.

Briar felt her throat clog and her nose sting with emotion. "Stop being so wonderful. It's extremely unbecoming of a dangerous rogue. You do have a dastardly, wicked reputation to maintain, don't you know?"

"Do I?" His lip curled in that smirk that never failed to

make her heart race. "Well, suffice it to say, *that* part of me only makes an appearance when anything of mine is threatened." His voice dropped. "Or when my favorite brat needs a new lesson."

Briar shivered. "Oh."

He swooped in to gather her up into his arms, and she gasped. He seized the opportunity to claim her mouth in a messy, voracious kiss, making her senses spin. When she was sufficiently bemused, he set her down. "Allow me, Prickles, to get to my second surprise."

He walked to the office door and locked it, which instantly made her breath come faster, and then he strolled over to a small storeroom at the back of the office. Briar swallowed hard as he removed what looked like a decent-sized bench from the space, lifting it back toward where she stood in the middle of the room, huffing from the effort. It must have been heavy.

"What is that?" she blurted, wide-eyed.

"Guess," he said. "Look familiar?"

The waist-high, oddly constructed contraption resembled something she'd researched and written about. The bench-like shape had carved legs and was fitted with handles and stirrups, including an angled padded top and side with cleverly placed cutouts. Her cheeks flamed.

"You made me a *Berkley Horse*?"

Jasper smirked. "With some Lady Ivy improvements. I took some creative liberty for comfort but mostly followed your descriptions. Shall we try it?"

She shook her head, unable to contain her laughter. "You are the strangest, most amazing man I have ever met. You are quite possibly the only earl in the world to buy a girl property, tell her she can do whatever makes her happy, even if it's to write bawdy fiction, and then you build her an intimate bench based on what she invented in a fictional story."

"I am rather exceptional," he preened. "Now get in position and lift your skirts."

The low command fell like hot honey on her senses.

"Jasper, it's the middle of the day," she whispered, scandalized, though the idea was unreasonably titillating. "Anyone could hear us."

"Then that all depends on how quiet you can be," he said. "Skirts, Briar. *Now*."

And that was how, as it turned out, Briar discovered that she could be very, *very* quiet with the right incentive while the love of her life took her to indescribable new heights, folded over a piece of naughty furniture she'd cooked up in her very imaginative mind. When he finally joined her in the throes of rapture and they collapsed in a sweaty, delirious mess, Briar could only smile happily.

"So," her very talented fiancé said, tucking her into his chest, after he'd ferried her boneless body over to the divan in the corner of the office. "What's the verdict?"

Briar chuckled. "If you ever decide you don't want to be Duke of Harwick or the owner of Lethe, you could become a carpenter. We would be so *rich*! London is full of curious couples who would welcome a *Lushing* Horse of their own." She grinned. "Lushing Trestle? Lushing Loveseat? The possibilities are endless."

"It's an excellent prototype," he agreed, nodding sagely. "But I think we need a few more physical experiments to be absolutely, positively sure of our design."

Unable to hide her smile, Briar pretended to think. "I think you're right. Straps and buckles might be a nice touch."

"I knew I loved that brilliant mind of yours," he said, kissing her soundly. "We didn't even try the other side."

"There's *another* side?" She stared at him and then the contraption, her eyes rounding with renewed interest. Suddenly, she wasn't so fatigued anymore. Giggling, she stood and dragged him toward it, though by the already erect state of him, he wouldn't be protesting too much. "No rest for the wicked, my lord."

And that was the reason servants reported the sounds of unhinged laughter coming from the office of the Earl of Lushing for a good few hours that afternoon.

Much later on, when a well-loved and starry-eyed Briar caught up with her friends at the last ball of the season, she couldn't help seeing a similarly joyful rapport between the couples.

It was incongruous and yet utterly unsurprising that something as small as joy could have an impact that was so powerful and far-reaching. Perhaps it wasn't such a revolutionary concept that pleasure was pervasive. Happier, healthier bodies meant happier, healthier minds.

All the Hellfire Kitties were proof of that, whether it was between a stone-hearted grump of a duke and a sassy French ballerina, or a scholarly paleontologist-turned-peer and an impulsive high-society darling, or a caber-tossing, uncivilized Scot and an unsociable animal lover. Or even Lushing and her: a rakish, dangerous earl with a heart of gold and a suffragist-heiress who wrote subversive literature.

They had each found meaningful unions with their partners who adored, respected, *and* desired them, and vice versa. The journey for each of them hadn't always been easy, nor was success ever assured. But it was in *choosing* to make that journey, no matter the outcome, that was the whole point. Love was a choice...one that they all made every single day.

In the words of the illustrious Jane Austen, it was half agony, half hope.

And in the words of Lady Briar Fairview, it was *always* worth fighting for.

AUTHOR'S NOTE

Dear Reader,

I can't believe we are at the end of the *Taming of the Dukes* series! Thank you so much for reading *Only Earl In The World* and joining Briar and Lushing on their journey. This one was inspired by *Drive Me Crazy,* which is another iconic 90s film (the whole series is based on 90s movies—did you catch the tiny nod to *The Cutting Edge*)? I had such a fun time with this story and was also so happy to come back to the most amazing friend group ever, the Hellfire Kitties.

As you know, I always hope to make my historical romance books as immersive as possible with authentic details. I am addicted to etymology.com and making sure words are period-appropriate (you'd be surprised at the root origin of some modern-sounding words), and I also love including actual people from the era.

While my heroine, Lady Briar, is a fictional suffragist, Viscountess Katherine Amberley, Millicent Garrett, and Dr. Elizabeth Garrett were real women from the Victorian era who fought passionately for women's rights. In 1860s England, the suffrage movement was in its early stages. The London National Society for Women's Suffrage was founded in 1867 and led by Millicent, who was only *nineteen* years old at the time! Many women lobbied, wrote articles, made speeches, and participated in local groups.

In 1870, Lady Amberley gave a lecture on women's rights, which drew the attention of Queen Victoria. Apparently, speaking about politics in public was unbecoming of a viscountess! The queen wrote this in a private letter to Sir Theodore Martin in 1870: "The Queen is most anxious to enlist everyone who can speak or write to join in checking this mad, wicked folly of 'Woman's Rights,' with all its attendant horrors, on which her poor feeble sex is bent, forgetting every sense of womanly feeling and propriety. Lady____ ought to get a good whipping." (Source: *Queen Victoria As I Knew Her* by Sir Theodore Martin, K.C.B.)

The queen clearly did not support the women's suffrage movement, which had to be disheartening for many Victorian women, who might have looked to her as a leader during the period. I did take some creative liberty in using the sentiments from the letter, since *Only Earl In The World* is set two years earlier in 1868. Nonetheless, it took almost sixty years before an amendment was passed in 1918 giving the vote to women who were over thirty, and it wasn't until 1928 that the voting age was made the same for both men and women.

Victorian views on a woman's role were rather strict. She was expected to care for her husband, her children, and their home, while her husband focused on business or politics. Marriage brought with it more rigid rules, and a wife was essentially the property of her husband. Upon marriage, anything she owned became his. In the *Taming of the Dukes*, I wanted my heroines to challenge and subvert these stringent rules and expectations placed on them by society, especially since my research showed that not all women followed the status quo. Certainly, the ladies mentioned above didn't let society's rules stop them. But there are countless examples of many intrepid women throughout history, and across cultures, who subverted traditional norms.

I loved that Briar and her friends were so sex-positive, and this mindset wasn't as modern or rare as it might seem. One of the interesting things I discovered in my research was an unpublished sex survey of women in the 1800s by Dr. Clelia Mosher, which asked questions about Victorian women's sexual habits, proclivities, appetites, pleasure, and partners. In this survey, a woman born in 1844 said sex was "a normal desire" and "a rational use of it tends to keep people healthier." Another claimed that if she didn't orgasm, it was "bad, even disastrous" along with "nerve-wracking-unbalancing if such conditions continue for any length of time." One of the women surveyed claimed, "when no orgasm, took days to recover." So, there were definitely women, including aristocrats, who pursued and valued pleasure.

On the naughtier plot points, the most famous of the "governess" sex workers was Theresa Berkley in Marylebone, who worked in the sex trade for almost fifty years until her death. She invented the Berkley Horse, a bondage rack where a man could get birched, among other things. As far as Lady Ivy's adventures, Briar's publisher, Theophilus Sebastian Judge, was a real person and the son-in-law of William

Dugdale, one of the most notorious publishers of erotic books in London. In 1869, Theo spent two years in prison for obscenity. Many publishers were imprisoned by the authorities, which was why so many authors in this subgenre, both male and female, were anonymous or went by pen names. For research, I read the erotic French novel, *Gamiani, or Two Nights of Excess* written anonymously by Alfred de Musset in 1833, a story about an insatiable French countess and her sexual explorations. She was rumored to be inspired by his lover, George Sand, a prolific female writer of the era, and fierce advocate of women's rights, passion, and free love.

While writing this story, I was fascinated by the dynamics between sexual identity and women's suffrage—both things on opposite sides of the spectrum but also rooted in the same philosophy that a woman should have autonomy over her own body, whether it was to vote for self-governance and protections, or to prioritize female agency and pleasure. Women's bodies—and human bodies—still remain inherently political. Mary Wollstonecraft, arguably the mother of modern feminism, said it best in *A Vindication of the Rights of Women* written in 1792: "Women, I allow, may have different duties to fulfil; but they are HUMAN duties, and the principles that should regulate the discharge of them, I sturdily maintain, must be the same."

Hope you enjoyed reading! Thank you for spending time with Briar and Lushing, and accompanying them to their happy-ever-after!

xo,

Amalie

ACKNOWLEDGMENTS

First and foremost, a huge thank you to all of YOU who took the time to read and review or send me personal messages about how much you loved the books in the series. I wouldn't be here without you. This book is for you.

Massive thanks to my very talented cover artist and designer, Rut Bisbe, who is an absolute superstar, and you should all go follow her on Instagram @ruisfree. She completely nailed this cover and made it look so perfect with the other three.

To my agent, Thao Le, as always, thank you for always being such an amazing advocate!

Special thanks to Angie Morgan and Wendy Higgins for their fabulous editing skills and being willing to read my very messy first drafts, including this one.

Thanks to my awesome PA, Mandy Jadick, who keeps making my books shine on socials, you're a gem! Also, she totally made me include that little easter egg at the start of the Author's Note. We giggled for a good ten minutes. Side note: surround yourself with people who bring laughter into your life.

Thank you to Danielle Hoegy for being such a fantastic cheerleader and spearheading the Only Earl In The World cover reveal.

To all the readers, reviewers, influencers, booksellers,

librarians, educators, close family and extended family, as well as friends who support me and spread the word about my books, my very sincere thanks. You are the best!

Finally, to my family, Cameron, Connor, Noah, and Olivia, thanks for being the joy in my world.

ABOUT THE AUTHOR

AMALIE HOWARD is a *USA Today* and *Publishers Weekly* bestselling author of "smart, sexy, deliciously feminist romance." Always Be My Duchess was one of *Cosmopolitan's* 30 Best Romance Books, and The Beast of Beswick was one of *Oprah Daily's* 24 Best Historical Romance Novels to Read. Her novels have received national awards, starred trade reviews, and have been featured in *The Hollywood Reporter*, *Screen Rant*, *Entertainment Weekly*, and *Seventeen*. She also writes young adult fiction as well as books for younger readers, which have been a Kids' IndieNext pick, a Target Book Club read, a Scholastic Book Fair selection, and on multiple high school state reading lists. When she's not writing, she can usually be found reading, being the president of her one-woman Harley Davidson motorcycle club, or power-napping. She lives in Colorado with her family.

Also by Amalie Howard

HISTORICAL ROMANCE

REGENCY ROGUES

The Beast of Beswick

The Rakehell of Roth

The Wolf of Westmore

DARING DUKES

The Princess Stakes

Rules for Heiresses

The Duke in Question

Any Duke in a Storm

TAMING OF THE DUKES

Always Be My Duchess

Never Met A Duke Like You

The Worst Duke in London

Only Earl in the World

FANTASY ROMANCE

STARKEEPER

The Starlight Heir

Queen of the Night Sky